THE LAST
LETTER

ENDORSEMENTS

"Compelling, evocative, shocking and true, *The Last Letter* is a wonderful debut from Bethan Marshall. She is a natural writer who brings her historical tale of men and women, politics and prejudice to vivid life."

MICHAEL BRACEWELL
British writer and novelist

"*The Last Letter* is a fascinating historical novel based on family papers passed down to the author Bethan Marshall. Part of its strength is found in Marshall's knowledge of the history, literature, politics, philosophy and theology of the times covered. A delightful read!"

REBECCA PIPPERT
Author and international speaker

THE LAST
LETTER

BETHAN MARSHALL

A
NOVEL

AMBASSADOR INTERNATIONAL
GREENVILLE, SOUTH CAROLINA & BELFAST, NORTHERN IRELAND

www.ambassador-international.com

The Last Letter

ISBN: 978-1-64960-413-2
eISBN: 978-1-64960-461-3

Cover design by Hannah Linder Designs
Interior typesetting by Dentelle Design
Edited by Katie Cruice Smith

Scripture taken from the King James Version of the Bible. Public Domain.

AMBASSADOR INTERNATIONAL
Emerald House Group, Inc.
411 University Ridge, Suite B14
Greenville, SC 29601
United States
www.ambassador-international.com

AMBASSADOR BOOKS
The Mount
2 Woodstock Link
Belfast, BT6 8DD
Northern Ireland, United Kingdom
www.ambassadormedia.co.uk

The colophon is a trademark of Ambassador, a Christian publishing company.

ACKNOWLEDGMENTS

I WOULD LIKE TO THANK my editor, Katie Smith. In the politest possible way, she suggested a major reorganization of the book, and it is all the better because of it. I would also like to thank my very patient husband, who read and reread endless versions during lockdown and, after, was always willing to discuss what I had written and provide endless support. My friend Rose Brougham also read various drafts of the book and acted as the perfect critical friend. Angela Wright and Michael Bracewell, who read the penultimate draft of the novel, gave valuable feedback. I would also like to thank my two daughters, who allowed me to portray a fictionalized version of themselves and also my great-uncle for his extraordinary story.

AUTHOR'S NOTE

THIS NOVEL IS BASED ON a true story. My great-uncle Fred was sent to the States because of an unsuitable love affair, and he wrote letters home to his sister Hilda. I first read these letters when my daughter needed to find a genuine historical source during her first year of doing a history degree. My father gave them to me.

The story haunted me and when, during the pandemic, I had to find something positive to do, I went back to them and started exploring the family history once again—but this time from a fictional perspective. So, the character of Niamh is imagined, as is Fred's friend in America, Niall. Hilda remained single until the day she died, although in the novel, she is married and an early suffragist. Yet what happens in the story, especially Fred's tale, is largely based on real events.

1

1907

Ellis Island, USA

"So, it's not quite what I was expecting. I mean, I wasn't expecting a welcoming committee, but I was looking for something a bit more friendly." Niall was looking around, over his shoulder and then back toward Fred. "There are just so many of us. You don't even really get a good view of the Statue of Liberty."

He caught a glimpse of the immense toga clad woman, shepherding her flock into the United States. "I wonder if we'll even all get in," Niall continued. "I've heard horror stories about people coming all the way across the Atlantic and being put on the first boat back. Something to do with their eyes."

Fred turned toward his companion of just three weeks, five days' crossing and then two more stuck on the boat waiting to be allowed to disembark. It seemed like so much more. Crammed together in steerage, you soon became intimate with those around you, bunkbeds all piled one on top of the other.

For the first couple of days, they'd been too sick to talk of anything. When they'd left Liverpool, it had been sunny and seemed calm; but once in the Irish Sea, it had become rough and rougher still as they passed the place they'd both once called home.

Fred had taken *Moby Dick* to read on the crossing. He'd chosen it deliberately, partly because it was long and written by an American— and that, after all, was where he was headed—but also because it was about a man escaping something and taking to the high seas. But as the boat heaved back and forth over the waves and the thought of reading anything felt sickening, he had begun to think it was a mistake. That and the way Ishmael seemed so isolated, cut off from everything on the land—alone in the middle of a vast ocean.

Two days in, though, he had begun to feel more human—physically, at least. It wasn't that the sea had become that much calmer but more that he had started to get used to the heave of the waves. Some people called it getting sea legs. Fred wasn't sure about that, but he had begun to feel a bit more like himself, as had the man beside him, Niall.

"Your eyes look all right to me," Fred assured him. "I think it's something to do with them seeming pink or lumpy. I don't know. I feel pretty healthy." He turned back. They were approaching Ellis Island.

It was small, dominated by a large building with four turrets. Meant to be just an entry point to the United States, the building took on the air of an adjudicator. *Are you fit or not? Are you healthy or infectious? Will we have to look after you or not? Will you sap our resources or add to them? Are you the kind of person we want mingling with those already here, or do we want to send you back? What quarrels do you have that you should have left behind?*

When finally given their turn to disembark, Fred noticed the face of the building loomed large, looking down on him as he was shuffled into a long line of people—children, parents, grandparents—all hoping that the United States would bring them something new. It seemed that they would be on the island a while, the queues of the hopeful snaking slowly forward.

Niall, still standing next to him muttered, "See what I mean? No one here to say, 'Grand, you're here. How was the journey? How are you doing?' You're just a statistic—and possibly not a good one, at that. We'll be here for hours. They have to check you medically and whether or not you have a place to go and everything. Honestly, if I didn't want to be here, I might just give up."

Fred wondered how much he himself actually wanted to be here— in America, on Ellis Island. The full weight of the decision he had made just six weeks ago suddenly weighed upon him. For all intents and purposes, this was a fresh start from his family, especially his father. He could put the past behind him, neatly package it up and leave it at home—his old home. Bury it. But of course, he was here was to bring that past with him, bring Niamh to America as well. He wanted a fresh start but with her by his side, and she wasn't here. *Niamh.*

As he edged forward, lost in a train of thought, he almost stumbled into the family just in front of him. The mother had a baby strapped to her with a shawl. Fortunately for her, the baby was asleep; but she had a toddler clawing at her skirt and a girl of about five who seemed exhausted and, so, tetchy with her tiredness. The mother, too, looked as if she could lie down right there on the floor, her face pallid and strained.

The husband seemed intent on being cheerful, keeping them all going with promises of what New York would be like. "It'll be grand. We've got a place to live in Brooklyn. It's small, but we can make do."

"But we spent all our money just getting here," his wife argued.

"I know, but they say that this is the 'land of opportunity.' I'll find something. Honest I will. We'll more than survive. We just have to get through this last bit, and then we're on our way. Isn't that so, Katy?" He ruffled the head of the small girl as they moved forward, the tired mother continuing to hold the baby, while watching the toddler and young Katy.

Fred pulled a face at the toddler and the small girl as they hid behind their mother's skirts. Fred peeked around and pulled another face, and the toddler began to smile. He stuck his fingers in the corners of his mouth and moved them up and down, sometimes smiling, sometimes glum. Katy began to laugh, but the toddler still glowered.

Fred looked around in an exaggerated fashion, one hand resting above his eyes. Katy laughed some more, and then Fred looked back at her putting both hands in front of his face only to reveal it again with great surprise. His hands enclosed it once more, and this time, he was frowning.

The toddler came out from behind her mother now. The mother looked over at Niall. "Is he always so good with children?"

"He's got some wee brothers back at home."

"I think he's a bit of a wee brother himself. Can we borrow him for the rest of the day?"

But at that moment, their paths diverged. Fred waved to Katy, blew her a kiss, and bowed, his arm sweeping up and then down nearly touching the floor, as the family was put into a separate queue. Katy waved goodbye to her new friend as her family merged into their line.

Now inside the building, Fred looked up. The hall that they'd entered was large with a balcony on either side of it and at the end. Everything about the interior was curved—curved ceiling overhead, curved windows within it, and more curved windows on the side. He wondered if this was the Americans' attempt to make everything seem less official, less bureaucratic. *Look, there are no sharp edges here; we are enfolding you in our warm embrace.* The problem was that the atmosphere he was beginning to feel did not seem so amicable. Although many of the people from the Baltic appeared to be getting through, there were others who were not.

"I'm getting nervous, and no funny faces are going to make me feel better," Niall said.

Fred laughed. "You don't need to worry. I'm sure it'll be all right."

"Yes, but that boy just got taken away." Niall nodded in the direction of two officials who were leading a boy out a side door. He looked about only fourteen, was thin and pale, and he was coughing. There were doctors scattered around who were checking whether or not you had a disease that might be contagious. It appeared that the boy had been one of the unlucky ones.

"Where's he going? They've marked him with chalk."

"I think they have a hospital on the grounds. Maybe there."

"Or maybe back home again. Look, is that his mother crying? Honestly, it makes you think that even if you know you're healthy, somebody will say you're not. Really, look, she's distraught. Can you imagine having your child taken away from you like that? It's dreadful. So much for compassion!"

Fred saw the woman sobbing as the boy left the hall. Someone, a woman, took hold of her and she crumpled in her arms. "I think they must be worried about consumption."

But that didn't excuse the matter-of-fact way the officials had dealt with the boy, or with the mother. They had come to America full of hope, and that hope was crushed in a simple dismissal of the boy from his parent. No embrace for them. No Niamh. He faltered.

"So, what's the first thing you will do when you get through?" Fred said too brightly.

"Such confidence. I suppose I'll try and find somewhere to live. My family has contacts in Brooklyn, so I'll try there and then go looking for a job. Not all of us have one lined up."

"Shopworker in Philadelphia. O, the joys," Fred responded sarcastically.

"Shopworker and a place to live, as well. Don't complain. You're bound to get in."

"I suppose. At least, I have to thank my Da for that, if nothing else."

"I never asked. How did he manage to organize it?"

"Some people we used to know came over a few years ago and heard of the job. I'm lodging with them."

"So, you know them?"

"I was incredibly young when they left, so it was my parents who knew them, honestly."

"You really don't like your father, do you? Even though he's set you up with a job and a place to stay?"

"Can you blame me?"

"Now, we're not going to get into that whole sectarian divide thing again; but she *is* a Catholic, and you *are* a Protestant. I'm just saying, it isn't easy."

"But it has to be about the person. If anything, she's from a better-off family than I. He never even met her, knew nothing about her. He just dismissed her, the whole idea of her. You're a Catholic, too, and he wouldn't have had the same reaction. He wouldn't have been thrilled, but he wouldn't have sent me to America."

"But you aren't wanting to marry me!" Niall quipped.

"I know. I know. I realize I keep repeating myself, but if you'd seen how angry he was . . . He was . . . What's that word Niamh used? Incandescent. That's what he was. Incandescent. The sheer rage."

"You know, it wasn't 'til about three days ago that I realized you were a Proddy."

"Really? Why?"

"Well, you kept talking about how you'd left everyone behind, and you had ten brothers and sisters and a girlfriend called Niamh. And you didn't actually tell me that whole sad story until a few days ago."

"I suppose."

"And you seemed a pretty decent sort of chap . . . "

"Careful . . . "

"To be honest, I don't think I've ever really gotten to know a man from the other side of the divide. Maybe they should stick the whole of Ireland on a boat and say, 'Get on with it. We won't let you off until you're sorted.' At least, we'd know the other lot were human."

"All except my father and maybe some of the die-hard Fenians and Orangemen!" Fred asserted.

"Maybe we could set them afloat on life rafts and leave them behind."

They both started to laugh as Fred clapped Niall on the back. "Can you imagine having a conversation like that at home? They'd have us both in irons. I think this American soil is already having an effect!"

"It looks like we're getting closer, and nobody's come and taken us off yet," Niall said hopefully. "I think this could be it."

The endless queue in front of them was getting smaller and smaller until finally they were there and a brusque official asked what they had put down on the manifest. They stated their names and occupations. And that was that.

Fred looked over at Niall, his companion of merely three weeks. "Well, we're in."

"We are, indeed."

"Remember to write and tell me your address. I feel I need to know somebody now that I'm here."

"Don't worry. I will. I have to share the crack with someone. I'll be going now, though, and getting a boat back to New York."

1905

IRELAND

Niamh sat in the staff room, hunched over the set of books she was supposed to be marking, and chewed on her pen. She opened one of the books. It had a picture of a woman in a chariot, one arm raised, hair flailing out behind her, reins held high. She noticed that there wasn't a horse to pull the chariot. The reins simply disappeared into the crease of the book. Drawing a horse was perhaps too ambitious for this eleven-year-old, but the rest was convincing. Underneath the picture was written *Boadicea, Queen of the Iceni* and then a brief explanation.

> *Boadicea was queen of the Iceni, and she fought against the Romans. Although she didn't win, she was very brave. She beat them all the way to London, but then she was defeated. She didn't wait for a man to fight. She just saw the need and did it for herself and the Iceni. She is buried under Liverpool Street Station.*

She put a large tick by the illustration and wrote at the end:

> *Yes, she was very brave. It just goes to show what a woman can do given half the chance. Her husband left his kingdom to her and didn't worry about finding a male heir. I think you need to say a bit more, though, about her various battles, like the one in*

Colchester. I think the folklore tradition is that she's buried under King's Cross, not Liverpool Street; but you ought to say it's not historically proven.

She closed Teresa's book and picked up another. This one was not illustrated. To be fair, she hadn't asked them to illustrate their homework, but evidently, Teresa had felt that the drawing might enhance her lack of historical information in a way that Ann-Marie, whose book was in front of her now, did not.

Ann-Marie described in some detail the rape of Boadicea and her two daughters before talking about her defeat at the hands of Suetonius, all of which was correct but somehow portrayed Boadicea as a victim rather than a triumphant warrior. Although Teresa's version was short, Niamh thought she had captured why the Victorians liked Boadicea so much. She was triumphant even in death, fighting off an army of oppressors.

Niamh enjoyed teaching Boadicea, also known as Boudica. She was, perhaps, the only figure in the history she taught that combined being a powerful woman with someone who fought off, at least for a period of time, an invading army.

She smiled. *You can be a suffragist and a nationalist, and here's the proof.*

"You're still marking those books? I left you with them half an hour ago, and you've marked how many? Two? Honestly, Niamh, you'll be here till midnight if you carry on at this rate." Erin, her ebullient, talkative friend, interrupted her train of thought.

"I was thinking about Boudica. She was a suffragist and fought for independence."

"Och, please no. We're not going to argue about that again, are we?"

"I was just thinking that you can do both," Niamh said tentatively. She knew what was coming, but she felt the need to have the conversation anyway.

"Look, I understand that it's important for girls to get an education. I'm teaching them, aren't I? But it won't do any of us any good if we can't rule ourselves," Erin said, exasperated. "Not even the men can get on, even with a degree. Things can be equal only if we get Ireland back for the Irish."

"Yes, but who knows if they'll make us equal, even if we get independence? I think they're all too happy with the way things are."

"I think you're wrong." Erin shook her head. "They know what it's like to be second-class citizens, and they hate it. That's why they want independence so badly. That's why I want Home Rule. So we don't have to kowtow to a government across the water who sees anyone who's a Catholic as someone less than equal."

"Can't we fight for both, though? You're right, of course, but we don't even get a say as women. And if they pay Catholic men less than the Protestants, they pay the women even less. I'm just as qualified as any man. I've even got a history degree! But because I'm a woman, I get less."

"But at least you work. Look at your aunt Siobhan," Erin fired back. "What a waste of intelligence. Only went to school so she could read and write, and because she didn't marry, your father has to look after her. And she is more than capable of working. And it's partly because of that your father was so keen to get you educated so you wouldn't be a drain on your brothers. So, you see, things do change!" she added with an air of triumph.

"I hardly think my father got me educated only so I wouldn't be a burden to my brothers! He is a teacher, too, you know. He believes in education passionately!" She was depressed that her family history should be used by Erin in defense of Irish nationalism, as opposed to women's rights, and infuriated at the way she misinterpreted her father's motives.

Niamh thought of him—his wonderfully disheveled form, patches on his jacket over crumpled trousers, surrounded by books. He often read aloud to the family—Dickens, the Brontës—lingering over the descriptions in his Irish lilt, telling the stories of Irish mythology or capturing the cadence of a Yeats' poem.

"He was reading *The Friendly Giant* to me before I could even speak. I mean, he's not like Oscar Wilde and 'arts for arts' sake,' but he's quite close. And," she snapped, "he certainly didn't educate me so I wouldn't be a burden to my brothers."

Erin was duly chastened, but she didn't alter her point of view.

"I know; I know. I was just trying to say that even if the men like being in charge, there are other incentives for giving women equality—even if they aren't particularly good ones."

Niamh smiled. "We're just going to have to agree to disagree."

It was almost certainly that conversation that had finally persuaded her to go to the suffragist meeting. She had been weighing the possibilities for so long, first this way and then that. Home Rule, independence, suffragism—all kaleidoscopically tilted in her mind. She understood that for Catholics, independence was preeminent. But then, hadn't women been oppressed as well? And so, she went to a meeting that was advertised in the window of the pharmacy near her home in Toombe Bridge.

The woman who welcomed her was tall, slim, and slightly formidable at first in her awkward, unyielding manner. Yet there was also a sense of certainty, a directness.

"Welcome to my home," she greeted Niamh. "My name is Hilda. Please come in."

"Thank you. I am Niamh," she replied hesitantly.

Following Hilda into the house, Niamh saw there were only three other women there, perched on the upholstered couch, the one comfortable chair, and a couple of dining room seats brought in from the room next door.

"I suppose we ought to introduce ourselves," said Hilda, "and say a bit about why we're here and what we hope to achieve. I'll begin." She took a deep breath. "I think I'm here because of my mother, not that she's a suffragist—far from it—but she should be.

"She kept having girls, but my father wanted more boys. They had me, and then a son, and then seven more girls until he had another son. Then they had one more just for good measure. I think they've stopped now. I do hope so. She's so exhausted that I look after the two of them most of the time.

"I think that's why I've become interested in the women's movement. It seems dreadful that a woman should have to keep on having children till she has her quota of boys. That and the fact that they don't have a say in anything. So why are the rest of you here?"

All of the women present were Protestants, except Niamh. Ann was a Quaker; and Lotte, like Hilda, was from the Brethren Assembly.

Ann, who seemed so unassuming, spoke first. "I know we're meant to be very democratic," said Ann. "But it's a democracy for men, not women. I'm here for the vote."

"I am, too," added Elspeth, a seemingly fiery Presbyterian. Her thick, auburn hair was pulled back in a tight bun, and her pale skin was flushed against the freckles on her face. "It would be nice if we had a bit more say in the church, as well. I'm sick of being told what's important for women by a lot of elderly men. It's absurd."

Hilda laughed. "I've just remembered that's the other reason I'm a suffragist. It's true. The men of our church decide everything. They decide everything from the money that runs the church to what we give for charity. And all we do is provide tea at the end of the service and discuss what we'll cook for dinner. The elders have all the power, and women are allowed to only watch from the sidelines. It's just plain wrong."

"You're absolutely right," chimed in Lotte, leaning forward from her upright chair, lace-up boots placed squarely on the ground. "In our church, it's the men who decide who needs charitable help. It's the men who speak in the assembly, so theirs is the only interpretation of the Bible that counts and so they're the ones who get to say what's right and wrong." Her hands spoke as much as her words as she waved them emphatically up and down.

"And of course, the men think it's their God-given right to do so," Hilda railed. "Honestly, it's like they never read the Bible. It's just full of women. Strong, powerful women who don't back down in front of men—and they're not all called Mary!" She laughed as she looked over to Niamh. "Look at Deborah and Esther and the Proverbs woman. Lydia even taught the apostle Paul."

This was new to Niamh—the arguments over what the Bible meant, the varying interpretations that anyone could have. It wasn't that she didn't question some of the stuff that she heard on a Sunday morning, particularly about women, but it was different. The priest had significant authority, and most of the service was just call and response, along with the ritual of the Mass. For Hilda, arguing about a passage of Scripture meant arguing with an individual, often her father. For Niamh, engaging in a debate was more like arguing with two thousand years of the Church's teaching.

She reflected on what had made her so keen on the suffragist cause. She spoke hesitantly at first, aware that her motivation was different.

"I realize it's ironic saying it was a man who made me come, but in my case, I think it was. My father always wanted to know what I was learning in school and always had something else I should be reading; and when we talked, he always listened to what I had to say. I mean, he often questioned it, too, but I always felt that he saw me as an equal. And as I went on, I realized that wasn't always true of everyone. In fact, it was very unusual. I suppose I want it to be less so."

The evening passed quickly with the women discussing their strategy and ways they thought they could make a difference.

Finally, Hilda stood and said, "I think we will end the meeting for this week. I think our Protestant men could learn a great deal from a Catholic like your father, Niamh, and I hope you'll all return next week."

As they were leaving, Niamh saw a photograph of a young man, amongst others, on the mantelpiece above the fire. It struck her. The young man, dressed in a suit, had two small boys clutching at his legs.

He had blond, curly, almost frizzy hair; but it was the expression that interested her. He looked wistful—if it were possible to look wistful in such pictures taken in a photographer's studio.

"I see you're looking at Fred and our two wee brothers." Hilda had stopped behind her.

"Yes, sorry. I didn't mean to stare. You're right. There's quite an age difference."

"There is. Fred's the older one," she said, pointing, "and that's Stuart and Henry. I have to say that Fred is like your father—not the teacher part, though he reads all the time and can't prize his head out of a book—but he listens to women—well, to me at least. So, there is hope."

Niamh didn't think about him again for at least a year. She was too busy with the group. At first, they simply drank cups of tea, airing their points of view; but later, after they had gotten to know one another better, they began to take more serious action. Niamh was put in charge of writing letters to the papers, while others started petitions.

And then, Fred turned up one afternoon, about a year after the group had started meeting. Hilda was in full sway, telling everyone about a talk given in Belfast by someone called Margaret Cousins, a leading activist. A knock sounded at the front door, and as Hilda was preoccupied, Niamh answered it.

"I see Hilda's in full swing again," he joked, his face breaking into a smile. "I just wanted to pick up the book Hilda promised me. It's

Around the World in Eighty Days. I think she has put it on one side for me to get. She was enthusing about it and said I had to read it."

He stopped as if seeing Niamh properly for the first time. "Sorry," he said. "I'm her brother, Fred." His manner was unassuming, laughing at his sister with a complete stranger before actually saying who he was.

Hilda joined them at the door. ""I see you met my wee brother." She laughed. "Hang on. I'll get the book. You will love it." She returned, handing the novel over to Fred before turning back to Niamh. "We swap books that we've enjoyed. I think Fred reads more than me. I struggle to keep up with him, and he has a job as well." She turned back to Fred. "Do you want to come in?"

"What, and have myself dissected by a load of women? No, thanks very much. I'll be getting off." And just like that, he was gone.

Afterward, though, he always found an excuse to call round, just when the meeting was nearly over, almost always to recommend a book to his sister. He was particularly fond of H.G. Wells—*The Time Machine, War of the Worlds, The Invisible Man.* But on one occasion, he recommended a book that she hadn't heard of—*The Secret Agent.*

"Are you sure I'll like it?" Hilda asked.

"Yes. It's written by Joseph Conrad, and it's written in English."

"I should hope so, or else, I couldn't read it."

"But he's Polish, and yet he's written all these novels in a language that's not his own, which is staggering."

"That is impressive, but it still doesn't mean I'll enjoy it."

"You will. It's about a man who runs an unsuitable shop in Soho with his wife, but secretly, he's an agent and gets asked to blow something up. I won't tell you any more. You have to read it. It becomes quite tense, but it's all written in this elegant prose. Even if you don't like it, I'll have someone to argue about it with," said Fred.

Niamh was interested enough to read the book herself and asked her father if he had heard of Conrad.

"Yes, I have. He wrote a book called *Nostromo*. I've got it somewhere." He got up and started scanning the shelves, stacked full of books in no particular order, for the volume. "It's a difficult read, but at the same time, absorbing, almost mesmerizing. It's the style in which it's written. Quite compelling. Who recommended him?"

Niamh lied for the first time to her father. She wasn't sure why she did, except that it was a Protestant man who had told her about it and that seemed different from a Protestant woman.

"One of the women in the suffragist group I go to. But it wasn't *Nostromo*; it was *The Secret Agent*."

"Well, she has good but demanding taste. I've not read it, so I'll be interested to know what you think of it. In the meantime," he said, having finally found the book high up on the shelf in their living room, "here's *Nostromo*."

When Fred came around the next time, Niamh had bought and read the book. "You're right," she said. 'It's tragic, really, blowing up his brother-in-law accidentally like that and then the whole family disintegrating. It's so sad." She hesitated. "And relevant, in a way."

Fred looked pleased that Niamh was joining in, understanding the novel in the same way he did. "I'm so glad you thought it was good. It does have something to say about violence. It tears people apart, and innocent people die as well as the guilty."

"Yes, in the end, it all seems such a pointless waste. The anarchist's view doesn't seem advanced in any way."

"Absolutely."

She noticed, then, that Hilda was looking at Fred and smiling. "Good to see the two of you are in agreement. I was impressed with it, too, if it's of any interest to either of you; and it was beautifully written, even though it's a grim tale. His prose is meticulous."

The following week, Fred arrived at the end of the meeting, when Niamh was about to go home and everyone else had left. Hilda, who clearly knew, was matchmaking after a fashion and had found an excuse for her friend to stay. She asked Niamh to check over a letter that she'd written to the papers. It was just long enough for Fred to appear after everyone else had gone. He had his two unruly, small brothers, Stuart and Henry, in tow but asked if he could walk her part of the way home. Almost despite herself, she agreed. What harm could it do to walk home with the three of them?

"This one is Stuart," said Fred as they passed through the gate outside the house. "And this one is Henry. He's the youngest and the most boisterous of all of us. I think he feels that unless he makes a lot of noise, we won't notice him. Isn't that right, wee Henry?"

"It's a pleasure to meet you both," replied Niamh, doing a mock curtsey. "A real pleasure. I've seen your photograph, and now, I'm seeing you in person." She looked up at Fred.

Henry tugged at Fred's sleeve. "You said I could ride on your shoulders. You promised."

"Of course, I did. Climb on up."

Fred lifted him up and then swung him onto his shoulders, each leg straddling the sides of his neck.

"Are you ready?" he shouted and started to gallop down the lane.

Henry laughed and started pulling Fred's ears up and down and then leaned over his head and tweaked Fred's nose.

"This horse isn't going to get very far if you keep doing that," Fred said. So, Henry stopped. Fred went off again up the lane, bouncing the boy up and down as he did.

Stuart started to shout, "It's my turn, my turn," until Fred took Henry down and gave him to Niamh.

"Look after him; he tends to run off," he said, and then mounting Stuart on his back, he galloped off into the distance before coming back.

"Her turn, her turn," said Henry. And without even asking, Fred whipped her off her feet and trotted up the road.

"Put me down! Put me down!" she cried, but she was laughing too much to make it sound serious.

"Your wish is my command, fair maiden." And when he let her down, he held her for a moment before looking straight at her, then turning toward his younger brothers. "Who's up for a second go?"

And that was it. Niamh remembered thinking that day only of the man with the tousled hair and boyish charm, who seemed to read everything that was put in front of him, instead of the enormity of what she was about to embark on. He could only ever walk her as far as the outskirts of Toombe. Everybody knew who was a Catholic and who a Protestant; and news, or gossip, or bigotry had a way of entwining you in such a tangle. It could happen so fast, you had to be careful, so very, very careful.

1900

IRELAND

Hilda would later be able to remember with stark clarity the actual day she became a suffragist. Of course, she didn't have a name for it then, but she understood the passion for which equal rights was being fought. The sensation of being treated unfairly and having nothing she could do about it burned inside her like a visceral force waiting to burst out and explode. It had begun with the death of her little sister.

Martha was her parent's sixth child, and up until she turned seven, she was full of the energy of a child that age. She was particularly good at hide-and-seek. There were endless chests into which she was just the right size to disappear, and she could stand frighteningly still behind coats and jackets, always remembering to cover her feet.

All that had changed, though, one February when she complained of a pain in her side. It wouldn't go away, and then she had become feverish. The doctor was called and diagnosed Martha with appendicitis. The only solution was for him to operate on the kitchen table. The poor child, lying there on the scrubbed wooden surface, became hysterical as she was asked to breathe in the chloroform. The doctor was as careful as possible, but a kitchen table in a farmhouse wasn't as clean as it should be. Martha lingered on for a week afterward but died from an infection. One minute, she was there, mischievous and laughing; the next, she was gone. Taken. Her body was laid out in a tiny coffin for people to come and pay their last respects, even though she had been on this earth only such a short span of time.

The funeral had been on a bleak, overcast day. Damp and cold seeped in to the very fiber of the coats and scarves they wore to keep warm. Sleet had blown across the lake as they trudged, across the muddy path, to the Assembly Hall. Fred had been only about fourteen, but he'd been allowed to go to the graveside. Hilda hadn't. The elders hadn't deemed it fitting.

"That wee coffin was placed in the ground," Fred had said. "And the dirt was thrown on top of it. And not a word from anyone—no tears. Nothing. No, that's not true. Da did groan just the once. Actually, it was more of a howl than a groan, coming from somewhere deep inside of him. But nobody came up to him to console him, even to say how sorry they were. They all just stood there, heads bowed. I suppose they must have been praying. You can't really tell. But it was the silence that followed. You could reach out and touch it. It was oppressive, unnerving."

Edith, Hilda's mother, was distraught. She was expecting again for the eleventh time, and her body was about to give out. The doctor had told her to take to her bed for the rest of pregnancy, which was four long months, and the whole weight of looking after the whole family had fallen onto Hilda's shoulders. She was enraged when she realized it was her responsibility alone.

But one day, Hilda found her mother, who was meant to be resting, scrubbing her father's shirts on a washboard in the scullery. Her fingers were red and raw and her face a pallid gray. Wisps of her once rich, blonde hair straggled about her brow, her eyes expressionless with sheer fatigue.

"You need to lie down," Hilda had chastised her mother. "I can do his shirts, or heaven forbid, he can do his own."

"Your father's not himself at the moment. He's grieving."

"And you're not? I'm not? Martha's brothers and sisters aren't? We're all grieving. And what's more, you're carrying his eleventh child. He doesn't seem to care. Look at you. You can barely stand."

"He does care. It's just that he doesn't say it."

"Or show it in any way. Come on. I'll wash his shirt, and you go upstairs and lie down."

Hilda fulminated as she cleaned her father's shirt, scrubbing down vigorously on a stain, thinking with every scrub of something she would say to her father when he came home. He interrupted her mid-flow.

"It's up to you now to look after us," Ross declared. "I've told the school. You've learned enough, and now you can help your mother."

As if she hadn't done anything before, Hilda thought. As if he couldn't help, too, as if learning was only of limited value. As if she, a fifteen-year-old girl, was to take on a household of twelve people, the cooking, the cleaning—everything.

"How can you say that? It's my schooling, and she's your wife. It's your baby. Aren't you going to do anything?" she shouted.

"The Scripture tells us women suffer in childbirth."

"Yes, but that doesn't mean we have to make sure they do. Or make sure every other woman suffers in the same way."

"Are you questioning God's Word?" Ross asked, his manner becoming threatening.

Hilda was angry, too. "Of course not. I'm only questioning how it's always so convenient for you and the elders to use it to put women down."

He stood rigid, spat out his words, wrath revealing itself in spittle. "The temerity of your accusation," he blazed. "The Almighty God told Eve in Genesis 3, 'I will greatly multiply thy sorrow and thy conception; in sorrow thou shalt bring forth children; and thy desire shall be to thy husband, and he shall rule over thee.' And you have the audacity to say that the elders and I just pick bits of the Bible for our own convenience? Shame on you. Shame. You should be asking me what you can do for your mother, not the other way around."

"Maybe," she cried, too enraged to back down. "But eleven times? It's too much—and all because you want another boy. You have only two, and that's not good enough. I'm sure Mother respects you, but I don't think ruling over her can mean that she has to wreck her body. It's just not right. She's just exhausted. If it wasn't enough giving birth, she's expected to wash everyone's clothes, cook, and look after all these children."

He towered over her. "So, you *are* questioning God's Word and, what's more, saying I'm the one to blame."

"No, no, of course I'm not questioning the fact that Eve was cursed. But I am questioning your interpretation of it."

"There is no room for interpreting the Scripture here, Hilda. The Almighty says that she will bring forth children in sorrow. That's a woman's role," he retorted, dismissing her response as if he had ended the altercation.

Hilda looked up at him defiantly.

"All it actually says is that she needs to obey her husband; and if her husband wasn't so taken with having boys, she wouldn't have to suffer eleven times!"

He raised his hand as if to violently hit her; but Fred came into the scullery, so he turned and stormed out, the door crashing behind him. Fred was always there when she wanted to cry; he was there just to listen. Fred was her main supporter. He was only fourteen but still old enough to realize that someone had to be there for her in a way she felt that her mother, in spite of everything, was only partially. Yet sometimes, it seemed, the only course of action was for him to deflect the abjectness she felt.

"I've just finished another Sherlock Holmes story," he said with a look that acknowledged he knew this was the last thing on her mind at that moment. "*The Sign of Four,*" he persevered, as she took a deep breath and started to calm down. "These stories always start with someone telling Holmes what the problem is, and then he follows the clues in an exacting fashion. But it's Watson who tells the story. Holmes never gets carried away. He's just logical and pieces the puzzle together until he gets ahold of the villain. And Scotland Yard doesn't help at all. They just seem dimwitted beside the great mind of Sherlock Holmes."

"It's a pity all men aren't more logical and unemotional," Hilda said bitterly.

"I know," said Fred, hugging a now-tearful Hilda. "But it's better to think of ones that are than be upset by those who are most certainly not." He hugged her once more. "Don't worry. He will calm down eventually."

"He might, but the damage has been done. He's taken me out of school to run the house."

"It can't be true! You mean we'll have to eat what you cook?"

A half-smile crossed her face before she replied, "It won't be too long before he says you won't go either. He'll have you working with Uncle Robin before you know it. Just you wait and see."

"As long as I have the time to read, I don't care. Reading gives you the chance to escape. Live someone else's miserable existence!" Fred laughed.

"Seriously, though. It'll be harder for you to really escape if you have to leave school."

"I'm sure God will find a way," Fred answered.

In the aftermath of the row with her father, Hilda went upstairs to check on her mother. Her father was there, and as soon as he saw Hilda come in, he rose to his feet.

"I will leave you," he said and walked out, head held high.

"He does mean well," her mother whispered.

"Are you actually going to defend him?" Hilda asked, incredulous.

"I told you he doesn't say how much he cares but shows it in what he does. Putting you in charge is his way of saying I matter."

"But it wasn't him. It was the doctor who said you had to rest, not him."

"And do you think he would have let me continue if the doctor hadn't said anything?"

"Yes, I do. He didn't let you stop when you were carrying Stuart. Why should he now?"

"Because he could see that I wasn't coping with things and he doesn't want to lose me as well as the baby. He does love me. I know he doesn't say it, but the fact that he wants me to stop is his way of telling me that he cares."

"Well, you could have fooled me. The only thing he said to me was that women suffer and that if I questioned it, I was practically being blasphemous."

"That's because he's angry."

"Yes. Very angry. At me!"

"It's not only you that he's angry with, though," Mother said, holding Hilda's hand. "You're the person standing in front of him, so of course, he's going to shout at you—and you make it so easy. You stand up to him and argue with him. Of course, he's going to yell."

"So, he doesn't believe all that stuff about Eve?"

"No, he does. But that makes him angry in a way as well. Can you imagine what it must be like for a man, believing that your wife must take all that pain and suffering and not be able to do anything to help or stop it?"

"He didn't seem very angry with Eve just now," Hilda fumed. Her mother squeezed the hand she was still holding.

"That's because you take everything at face value. Had it ever occurred to you that he's angry with God for taking Martha and even more furious that soon it may be me? He's doing the only thing he knows how to do to look after us, and that's to provide. He's putting a great deal of trust in you asking you to take charge at home."

Hilda sighed. "Why didn't he just say that then, instead of preaching at me? I still don't think it's my job. And what's more, I don't think it's yours either." She looked at her mother's pale face.

"Why do you always explain his point of view so much better than he does?"

"Because I have been with him for nearly twenty years, so I understand him a bit better than you do. And despite what you might say, I love him."

"It still means I won't go back to school."

"I know, but you *have* been there longer than anyone else in the family. He did actually let you stay an extra year, so don't be too harsh with him." Mother closed her eyes as Hilda bent over and kissed her.

After their argument, her father seemed to withdraw from life. He still went to work at the small cement business he had started with his brother Robin; but he didn't speak much to Robin, and he didn't speak to his children at all. When he came home at night, he demanded his food and then sat in a corner by the fire studying his Bible.

The only place he did speak was at the Brethren Assembly, deflecting all his grief, as her mother kept reminding Hilda, into the Good Book. Sunday after Sunday, it was her father who preached, typically on the book of Job.

"God," he said, "could be with you, even though He let tragedy strike." He poured over difficult passages where God and the devil argued over the fate of Job. And he reminded them that Job remained patient throughout his trials. Hilda struggled, though, to see her father's taciturn silence as God-fearing patience.

Two, maybe three years later, her father had still dominated everything about her life and her mother's, too. Her mother had eventually given birth to another son, Henry, but having eleven children was too much for her. She had seemed to disappear, noticed only by Hilda. Ross seemed to notice only the boys. This was when he had paid for the photograph of them that now sat on the mantelpiece in Hilda's front room. He had packed them off to a photographer, all the way to Belfast, dressed up in their Sunday clothes.

"I have to have a record of you fine young men," he had said, glowing with paternal pride.

"What about having one of all your children?" Fred had asked.

"It's far too expensive to buy train tickets for ten of you to go to Belfast. The three of you will be grand, and we'll keep the negative so that you can all have a copy if you move away."

"I couldn't help feeling it was all wrong," Fred had told Hilda on his return. "There I was, standing there all stiff and starchy, and none of the rest of you were there. Who knows what'll happen to us all? Of course, I want to have a photo of Stuart and Henry, who, by the way, were dreadful—well, no, not dreadful. But certainly hard to contain until the photographer disappeared under that blanket-type thing over the camera. They were really spooked. And I kept thinking that you have a point. It's not men who matter; it's women, too. The whole thing made me furious, yet sad at the same time. Angry at my father. Sad because of the wasted opportunity and because of Martha."

Hilda experienced her first glimpse of freedom when her father decided they needed more money. So, Hilda was sent to work for a few hours a week in the pharmacy that had just opened. In addition to medicines, they sold soaps, perfumes, and creams—items, Ross believed, women would want, so it wouldn't be too demeaning to work in a shop.

When Hilda got her first pay package, Charles, proprietor and pharmacist, said, "I've worked out how many hours you've done and paid you the full amount."

"What do you mean the *full amount?*"

"Well, most shopkeepers would pay a woman less than a man, but I don't think that's fair. So, you get exactly the same as if you were a man."

"Thank you," she said, somewhat taken aback.

"You don't need to thank me. I'm doing only what I think everyone should do. Paying the same wage for the same work."

"Well, thank you for being such an enlightened employer, then," Hilda said gratefully. "I can't believe that my father has told me to work for a suffragist! He wouldn't like it, that's for sure."

"I'm not sure if I can be one as a man, but I do go and listen to Margaret Cousins in Belfast. She's a powerful speaker."

"I haven't heard of her," Hilda admitted.

"She's one of the leaders of the suffragist movement," Charles replied.

"I'd love to hear her speak."

"The next time she's speaking, you can come with my sister, Emily, and me if you want."

"It'll mean telling some white lies, but I'd love to," Hilda answered with enthusiasm.

It wasn't Charles' attitude toward women that eventually won her heart; it was his gentleness. He was kind to his customers, so concerned about their ailments, even the ones that seemed flimsy or invented from hypochondria. She wondered if he had been around if would Martha have died of her infection.

That was how she had first become interested in him, she confided to him on the way back from a meeting in Belfast. His sister, Emily, was there, too; but she kept her distance, aware, Hilda now realized, that her brother liked her.

"Could you have prevented the infection?" she asked Charles.

"I don't know, honestly," he answered.

"It was such an awful time. My mother was expecting her eleventh child, and so my father took me out of school to help run the house. I was only fifteen myself. It was hard."

Charles listened intently but didn't speak, his silence urging Hilda to continue.

"I have to admit, I was so angry with my father. He turned himself into a martyr, and it didn't seem to occur to him that my mother was so frail and grieving, too." She stopped suddenly, her voice beginning to break. "I'm sorry. I haven't spoken about this to anyone except my brother Fred."

He gently squeezed her hand. "And are you still angry?"

"I think I got too worn out to maintain the level of rage I felt. It's funny, really. My mother always defends him, says the reason he made me leave school was to help her—which, I suppose, is true to an extent—but he definitely prefers his sons to his daughters. You know, he has never thanked me for what I did. I know we're not supposed to look for gratitude, but just a simple acknowledgment would be nice."

"So, does Fred get on better with him, then?" Charles asked.

Hilda smiled. "He's far too loyal to his big sister. Besides which, I don't think he is too fond of the rants from the God of the Old Testament. Every Sunday, he hears about the wrath of God just waiting to judge us all."

"Instead of a God Who wants to save us."

SO, CHARLES FELL FOR HER plight, she for her savior. It wasn't an unequal marriage, though, with Hilda dependent on a man. She had too much of her brother's feistiness, his strength. She wasn't one who would submit to the role of women as society saw fit. She would fight for a new one and have her husband fighting by her side as she did so.

4

SUMMER 1906

IRELAND

Fred knocked on Hilda's front door and then hesitated as he heard voices talking animatedly from within. He had anticipated that Niamh would be there as she had said she would be coming over and could see him that evening, but he hadn't expected anyone else.

As he waited for the door to be answered, he tried desperately to think of a legitimate excuse for his presence and came up with nothing. He didn't have his small brothers with him, and he hadn't brought a book he could talk about or exchange. Those were the two things he typically relied on to explain his visit—other than the real reason. Niamh.

Hilda answered the door. Facing away from those inside, her expression was one both of surprise, exasperation, and a mild look of panic.

"Fred! How good to see you. I'm glad you've come to take that thing to our parents."

Fred looked blankly at her. "What . . . Oh, yes. Of course. The thing." And then toward Elspeth and Ann, he said, "I am so sorry to interrupt your meeting."

"Nonsense. There was no meeting. We were just here to encourage Hilda and Niamh to come with us next Wednesday to hear Margaret Cousins," Elspeth said, grabbing Hilda once more by the arm. "Please, do come with us," she pleaded. "Margaret Cousins is going to organize a large rally in Belfast, and she's going to give some of the details in her speech."

"Yes, do come," begged Ann. "Lotte has already said that she can come, so that just leaves you two. It would show solidarity as a group if we could all go."

"I feel I'm somewhat in the way." Fred laughed, shifting uncomfortably from one foot to the other.

"Nonsense," said Elspeth, picking up her bag. "Men are more than welcome. You know Charles is a regular attender at rallies. And I'm working on William. Perhaps you can persuade your sister to come and, of course, Niamh. She has no excuse as she is still on holiday."

"I will try," promised Niamh, glancing nervously over at Fred, "but, strangely, I seem to be busier in my holidays than I am when teaching. My mother has me doing all sorts of chores to keep me hard at work—mainly, keeping an eye on my younger brothers and sisters. But I will ask. If not, I rely on you both to take down all the details of the rally and tell us all at our next meeting."

"That I will," said Elspeth. "That I will. And don't you forget now, Fred, it's the men we're trying to persuade. You seem to be coming to a lot of our meetings," she added archly. "Or, at least, the end of them with your books and reading and wee Henry and Stuart. Maybe you should come at the start." She looked at Hilda and then pointedly at Niamh, who was trying to look as neutral as she could but was turning a pretty shade of pink. "Well, I must be off."

"And so must I," said Ann, putting on her hat and touching Niamh's arm lightly "Goodbye. And if we see either of you next Wednesday, it would be splendid; but if not, we will commit the details of the rally to heart and tell you all about it at the next meeting."

"I look forward to it," said Hilda.

She stood in the doorway and waved goodbye. Closing the door, she let out a cry of despair. "I am so sorry. I had no idea they were coming over, and now, it looks as though Elspeth has worked something out and . . . "

"And Ann," added Niamh. "What are we going to do?" She looked crestfallen.

"I will talk to them. Don't worry. I won't tell them everything. Just a light flirtation on your part, Fred."

Fred straightened his shoulders and breathed deeply. "On this one occasion, I don't mind that the man comes out badly. We are an undisciplined lot and treat, far too causally, the feelings of women. Blame us all for everything." He winked.

"I don't think I'll go quite that far, but thank you. We will just have to be more careful, I think—particularly if Elspeth and Ann are suspicious. This is no time for joking, Fred. We will have to be more discreet."

Fred looked duly chastened, realizing the severity of the situation. "I know; I know. But I trust you, Hilda, and you will sort it out." He looked across at Niamh, his expression softening as he saw the anxiety written across her face. He held her hand tightly. "It will be all right."

"Let's hope I can," said Hilda, intently fixing her eyes on both of them. "But in the future . . . You will have to think about what you're doing."

Fred and Niamh exchanged an apprehensive glance at each other and then looked back at Hilda.

"We know," they both said simultaneously.

Silence lingered for just a minute. As if to break the pause, Hilda asked, "By the way, what was it that you wanted to tell us, Fred? You sounded so keen when you dropped in on your way to work."

"Of course, I'd almost forgotten. Well, not really forgotten but just momentarily delayed." He was relieved that he could share good news away from what had just happened. His face broke into a smile. "I can tell you one thing, Niamh. You won't be able to go hear Margaret Cousins—and not because you will be tied up looking after your younger brothers and sisters. You will be coming with me to the north Antrim coast."

Niamh gasped. "Giant's Causeway?"

"Giant's Causeway. My father has entrusted me with a client who lives in Port Rush, and I have to see him next Wednesday. I thought we could spend the day there, far away from everyone we know."

"That would be wonderful," exclaimed Niamh. "Wonderful. But we still have the problem of how I am going to get there without anyone knowing. It's fine for you—you have an excuse. But where will my family think I am? I'm on holiday, so I have no reason to be away from home."

Fred turned to Hilda. "That's where you come in. I was hoping you could find some reason for Niamh to be here."

"I'm sure I can. There is always something that the suffragists need doing. And now, I think you need to go, Fred. Niamh, you need to stay on longer, in case the neighbors start talking as well. We'll work something out."

Wednesday soon came, and they set off early. At Toombe Bridge Station, they stood at opposite ends of the platform and got on the train in separate carriages, hoping that if they were recognized by anyone at the station, they would not be seen together. Fred did see someone who worked with his father and Robin. He nodded an acknowledgment; but the man got off at the next stop, and Fred breathed a sigh of relief. The train steamed its way through the next few stops until they arrived at Antrim, where they had to catch another train up to the north coast.

Both started to make their way to the center of the platform, searching out for people they might recognize. They saw no one amidst the crowd, some heading toward Belfast while others were heading up the coast. As the train drew in, they took a fleeting glance at the people around them and stepped into an empty carriage together. They were utterly alone. A sense of anticipation hung in the air as they sat side by side, staring at each other.

Breaking the silence, Niamh said, "I love the Antrim coast. The sea is quite untamed, and in winter, it roars in over the rocks. I went up there once with my family, and my father told us the story of Benandonner and Fionn mac Cumhaill."

"The two giants who made the causeway."

"The very same. Well, actually, only one—Fionn mac Cumhaill." She looked so pretty sitting there, her dark hair tucked away in a loose bun at the nape of her neck, her face animated at the thought of telling a tale.

"But he got scared of Benandonner, didn't he? So, he stopped building it or something because the Scottish giant was so big, he thought he couldn't defeat him," Fred stated.

"Yes, but the story doesn't end there." She laughed. "Typical of a Proddy to think that the Irish were scared off by the Scots."

"Be very careful what you say." He nudged her in the ribs.

"In a way, you're right." She poked him back. "It wasn't Fionn who defeated the giant. It was his wife. Well, it was her idea that defeated him."

"Go on, then." Fred leaned back on the seat and listened.

"Well, when Benandonner heard of Fionn mac Cumhaill's failed attempt to defeat him, he thought he would use the causeway to go to Ireland and beat Fionn once and for all."

"That's what I said," Fred protested.

"Ah, yes, but then Fionn's wife, Oona, heard of the plot; and being a canny, Irish woman, she told Fionn to dress up as a baby. So, when Benandonner came stomping along the causeway cursing and shouting for Fionn, he came upon a basket with an immense baby in it. 'If that's the size of the baby, what must his father be like? Too gargantuan for even me to fight,' he said, horrified, and ran as quick as he could all the way back to Scotland. All that brawn and fighting muscle reduced to nothing by his wily wife Oona," said Niamh triumphantly.

"I see," Fred said, conceding. "My plodding, somewhat dimwitted Scot, who thought a bearded giant was a baby, was taken in by a clever woman."

"Precisely." She grinned.

"The Irish legends are full of strong women," she added. "Take Maeve. She was a warrior queen of Connaught."

"I think I've heard of her. I'm not sure."

"They don't teach you Protestant boys properly, do they?"

"They didn't teach me much at all in school," Fred confessed. "I found books quite by chance."

"Yes, but these legends started off as oral traditions and are Irish in their very bones."

"So, they don't teach them to us," Fred said somewhat disconsolately. "So, come on, tell me about Maeve, then. I'm all ears."

"Well, she had a fight with her husband, Ailill, over a white-horned bull."

"A fight over a bull? Not the typical cause of a quarrel between man and wife."

"But it was important, you see," said Niamh, beginning another story with a sense of relish, "because owning it meant that he was deemed to be the superior and wealthier one of the partnership."

"I thought you said the legends are full of strong women."

"I did," Niamh went on, "because Maeve heard of this other bull, which was brown and meant to be better, and she thought, *If I get the brown bull of Cooley,'*—that's where it was from—*'people will think I'm better than Ailill.'* So, she set about getting it. But then she was warned by a prophetess that if she went after the bull, she would be doomed."

"I'm assuming she ignored the prophetess."

"Now, you're beginning to understand."

"Go on."

"Well, the prophetess has said that Connnaught's army would be defeated by the Ulster army," continued Niamh.

"And the Ulster army is on the side of Ailill?"

"Cooley is in Ulster."

"I see," said Fred, slightly losing the plot.

"Anyway, Maeve sends her warriors into Ulster, and meantime, the Ulster army are also struck down by a curse."

"There are a lot of curses around." Fred laughed.

"But," Niamh went on, ignoring the interruption, "one of them wasn't cursed, and he was called Cú Chulainn. He comes into quite a few of the legends. Anyway, he's very brave, and he holds the army from Connaught at bay. But then his old friend appears, and he's fighting for the queen. Cú Chulainn is shocked, but he fights him, nevertheless. They fight, and they fight, each one wounding the other. They fight for three long, terrible days. And Cú Chulainn is nearly dead from his injuries and overcome with exhaustion, but in the end, he wins. Then the curse on the Ulster army is lifted, and they come and defeat the army from Connaught."

"I thought you said this was a story about a strong woman."

"Ah, but it is."

"How? It's been all about fighting warriors so far."

"Because," Niamh, smiling, corrected him, "while once again the men were fighting with derring-do, Maeve got the brown bull and with it defeated Ailill's white-horned bull, and so she triumphed after all."

The train jolted to a stop, and Fred put out his arm to stop them both from lurching forward. He looked into her animated eyes and kissed her. The train jerked once more and broke them apart.

"I love the way you tell those tales. I'm sure if someone else was telling them, they would sound very different."

"Nonsense."

He paused. "I love Oona and Maeve just the way I love you."

They kissed once again, lingering until the train drew into Port Rush.

Niamh enjoyed the seafront while Fred met the man to talk business, and then they went to the Causeway. They walked hand in hand down the steep slope in the sunshine and came out at the base, huge hexagon pieces of rock followed by much smaller ones, all perfectly formed like some giant puzzle. They tried walking along part of it, but Niamh kept slipping over the smooth rocks so Fred helped her, his hand around her slender waist guiding her over the stones as she lifted her skirt and petticoat so as to not let them get in the way. Niamh almost fell, and Fred, in clutching her, had brought her toward him; and they kissed once more.

"I love you, too," Niamh whispered. "You're my Cú Chulainn."

Later, walking up along the hill at the side of the Causeway, Fred looked out along the coast. The bay swept round to the left, over the Causeway and on. He could see Donegal far over, almost disappearing on the horizon behind it, the sea a translucent gray flecked with white.

"You can almost see the shadows of all those ancient people with a view like this."

"And you can feel their warrior blood when it's stormy. It's part of the haunting beauty of the place—those wild, strange, magnificent Celtic tales."

They sat on the cliff for some considerable time, Niamh's head resting on Fred's shoulder, neither one speaking. They stayed, not until the sun set but almost, as the sky became a darker shade of blue, the clouds lengthened, and the breeze began to pick up. Then they wound their way back down the path and up from the causeway to a bus, which would take them to the station and home to Toombe.

SCHOOL BEGAN AGAIN IN SEPTEMBER, and that made it simpler to meet without being detected. Fred did still call at Hilda's; but more frequently, they met in Belfast, anonymous in the crowds. Often, they would stroll down the streets hand in hand, simply talking about their respective days. Once or twice, they wandered around J. Robb and Co. department store, fascinated by the wealth of merchandise on offer, particularly as the days grew colder and they headed toward Christmas. Niamh chose a scarf for Fred's mother, and Fred recommended a book for her father, *The Turn of the Screw*, because he enjoyed a chilling tale at Christmas.

"It's such a shame that we can't tell them that our choices were inspired by each other," complained Fred as they sat in the Foster Greens tea rooms when term started again in January. "I mean, look around. Can you spot who's a Catholic and who's a Protestant sitting here? No, you can't. I mean, is that man over there, the one in the hefty, black coat a Protestant or Catholic? There is no way of knowing, unless you asked him; and even then, he might equivocate, wondering why you were asking him."

He added milk to his tea. "You know," Fred said, stirring his cup far more than was necessary, his mind far from the action of his hand. "I can't even ask your father what he thought of his Christmas present.

I would have liked to ask him if he really thought there was a ghost haunting the house, or whether he thought it was two wicked children, or even that the governess was going mad. But I can't because he mustn't know of my existence." He put the teaspoon down with a clatter. "What *did* he think, by the way?" he added, almost as an afterthought.

"I think he thought that the governess was driven insane," Niamh replied. "But I'm not sure." She sighed. "You're right enough, though. No one has a label printed on their foreheads. Still, some people do wear crosses. And they are different, aren't they? You just have a cross with no one on it—the resurrected Christ rather than the sacrificial One."

"All right, then. There are some external differences; but I don't wear a cross at all, and you don't often. Look around, and you can't tell." He drank the tea, which was slightly too hot, and burned his tongue. He winced.

The tea room was crowded, the windows misting up from the bodies within. Another young couple sat down to order, the man helping the woman remove her damp coat and hat. She was smiling at the man, laughing at something he had said.

Fred turned to Niamh, lowering his voice. "I mean, how do we know that couple over there is not the same as us, coming here out of the rain and away from interfering parents? A young love, no longer taboo." He gazed wistfully at the couple in a way that had now become familiar to Niamh, his thoughts a long way from the object of his regard, his mind fixed on his present troubles.

She reached across the table and clutched his hands, not speaking. Breaking his stare from the man and the woman, Fred looked back at Niamh and turned her hands over in his own, holding them tenderly and squeezing them back. Then, as if shaking himself back into a more cheerful mood, he said, "I haven't asked you how your first day back at school was. Aren't you doing Boadicea again?"

She laughed, holding his look, which was both genuinely interested and loving. "Yes, yes, I am. I don't know whether to curse her or celebrate her."

Fred looked genuinely confused. Niamh laughed again.

"Well, if I hadn't been teaching her before, I wouldn't have argued with Erin. And if I hadn't done that, I wouldn't have ended up going to a suffragist meeting. And if I hadn't gone to that particular house, I would never have met Hilda. And if I hadn't met Hilda, I would never have met you. So, you see, Boadicea is both a curse and a cause for celebration."

Fred leaned across the table and kissed her.

Winter slipped by, and spring was hesitating to put in an appearance; it was still cold and raw. The Grand Hotel in Belfast loomed large and impressive, its pointed dome in the corner looking down on the trudging passersby, gray sludge from recent snow still on the pavement.

Fred looked down the street anxiously, and then he saw her scurrying along toward him, her hat slightly askew with dark curls spilling out underneath, her coat wrapped tightly around her as she held her battered briefcase to her chest, picking her way through the puddles and slush. As she came toward him, she smiled, her cheeks a fresh pink against the cold. *Niamh.*

"So, to what do we owe this very important occasion? Dinner at the Grand Hotel. I had to think of all sorts of reasons why I would be out so late," Niamh said, slipping her arm through his and hugging him to her as they walked up the stairs into the lobby. Fragmented light shone from the vast chandeliers casting shadows over the bustling crowd beneath.

"You know, this hotel got its name from Grand Central Station in New York. The site was originally going to be a railway terminal like the one there, and the name just stuck," said Fred in a cheery tone, not answering her question. "Will we walk up the stairs or try out the lifts?"

"I think the stairs will do. Lifts unnerve me. I'm not sure I would like to be stuck in one of those. They look very pokey. Also, I'm not convinced the power won't suddenly cut out, and we'll plunge down the lift shaft." She shuddered.

"Honestly, they are completely safe. You have a very morbid imagination. But the stairs it is." He grabbed her hand and led her up the stairs to the restaurant.

"I have a table in the name of Anderson for dinner here at seven," Fred said to the somewhat austere maître d' standing behind a desk.

"Certainly," he replied. "Follow me." And he ushered them through the tables, past an intimate pair who seemed oblivious to all around them, a table of besuited business men raising their glasses, and a family gathering for what appeared a celebration until they reached the table for two, which was theirs.

"Here we are," said the maître d'. "A waiter will be over shortly." He pulled out the chair for Niamh, letting Fred seat himself, nodded, and turned back toward his desk.

Niamh fixed Fred with a stare. "Well, this is all very lovely, but, again, why are we here?"

"What would you like to drink?"

"Fred!" Niamh looked at him as if he were a child misbehaving at the back of her class.

"I will have . . . Let me see," he said, perusing the menu a little too deliberately, humming as he did so.

"Fred! Honestly. What exactly do you want to ask me?" she asked, mischievously, laughing as she did so. "It can be only one thing. So, come on, ask me."

Fred put down the menu.

"Maybe I won't ask you now. Perhaps I've changed my mind. Who would want to be tied to a woman who knew what you were going to say before you'd even said it?" He grinned at her. "I mean, I had it all planned. Take you somewhere fancy, wait till pudding, and then sweep you off your feet. But now . . . "

"Now?"

"Well, I mean, you're almost asking yourself, putting words in my mouth—to say nothing about impatience." As he said this, he reached into an inside pocket in his jacket and pulled out a small opal ring. "But since you are that impatient—and, might I say, almost nosy rather than just plain curious—and since you do know what I am thinking—sometimes before I've even thought it—would you, Niamh, do me the honor of becoming my wife? And please don't say no," he added hastily, "because otherwise, I have just spent a fortune on a ring and dinner. And I really can't afford it."

"Of course, I will say yes." She laughed. "Of course, I will!" Her face fell. "But now, we have to tell our parents."

"We could go to Londonderry or Belfast," Fred said, storming off down the road. "Anywhere. We could just run off and elope—just me and you—and leave the lot of them behind." They had decided to tell their parents separately but at an appointed time so that they would both hear the news together in a way. It was an agonizing decision but had to be done, and now they had to deal with the results.

"We can't live anywhere in Ireland," Niamh said as she almost ran to keep up with him. "The same problems would be there. Go somewhere in the North, and it would be impossible for me. Your father and all his business contacts would be bound to find us and, who knows, get the Orangemen onto us. And in the South, you just wouldn't survive. Some Fenian would discover us, and that would be that."

"I don't think my father is that bad—definitely the most dogmatic man I know and probably sectarian, but the Orangemen is going a bit far. I take your point, though. What about Scotland, then? We could take a boat over from Larne or maybe go to Liverpool."

"It'd be the same. Liverpool is almost as divided as we are, and I think it's the same in Scotland. Can you imagine you're going to the kirk and me a Catholic church? I can hear them saying, 'They think that their pope is a man of God, that he speaks with a Divine infallibility; but he's the antichrist, and he leads people to damnation.' Just like your father."

Fred slumped. "He preaches it as well. He gave a sermon recently on the Parable of the Sower. Catholics didn't come out too well."

"Why? What did he say?"

"Well, they were like the chaff—not even the wheat that was sewn too shallow that withers and dies. No, it was the chaff. And he said, 'The wind blows, and the wrath of God will come upon them.' And that was that. He thinks you're like the Pharisees, too. And the book of James—works."

"Honestly! I could tell him a thing or two. God loves good works. Really, He said that. Your father's distorting everything. He just doesn't know any Catholics. Has he ever sat down and even had a conversation with any of us? I don't suppose he even employs a Catholic or does business with one. He honestly believes that the charity of the Church is nothing more than pharisaical—that good people confess when they've done wrong and work hard to do right makes us just chaff."

"I think we're missing the point arguing with my father about theology. Works are only half the problem. Wait till you get him on communion. Mass. He thinks you're cannibals dressed up in religiosity, eating the body and the blood." Fred was deflated.

"We could sit here till night follows day and get nowhere." A note of anger crept into Fred's voice. "And it has to be said that your father—reasonable man though he might be—said no as well; and you were so certain he would come around with a little persuasion, but he was just as intransigent. So much for his culture and letters. What's that book you say he likes? *Hard Times*? And how it's all about the imagination not just facts. Why couldn't he use a bit of imagination instead of the facts? And what about him saying everyone should read more so they can think for themselves? Wasn't that what he wanted? Well, you were thinking for yourself, and he said don't!"

Niamh felt the need to defend him.

"It was the shock more than anything. He kept saying, 'Why, when you realized that he was serious, didn't you stop it? Why are you telling us of this only now? Why did you let your feelings rule over what you knew was right? Why didn't you let your head rule your heart?' And it didn't matter how much I said I wanted something different, something that would allow a Catholic and a Protestant to be together; he wouldn't budge. He kept saying the same points over and over again, and in the end, I left. My poor mother just sobbed in the corner. I could hear them talking right through the night. Arguing, really. I have never heard them like that. It was awful." Her voice cracked. "I'm so sorry."

"I'm sorry, too," Fred admitted, looking now at the forlorn figure beside him. "I am. I just can't think what to do. There seems no way around it. Do you really think he won't change? All that talk of the importance of education. Is there really no way he will think differently once the shock has worn off?"

She sat down. It was getting cold. The days were beginning to lengthen but only just, and a wind was blowing up from Loch Neagh a few miles away as night began to close in on them. Sitting down beside her, he put his arm around her as she leaned into his shoulder.

"I don't. I really don't. For all his talk of it, he thinks it's important that Catholics are taught by Catholics."

"Why?"

"Because even if they're studying someone he loves, like Dickens—he really believes most of what Dickens says is right—but he'll add that maybe because he's a Protestant, there aren't many Catholics in his books. And he doesn't think that, if you're a Protestant, you'll say there are no Catholics in his books. I've heard him too often saying, 'You just need someone to point that out, and you're not going to get that if your child is being educated by a bunch of Protestants. For them, it's not relevant. They'll just look at what he is saying and not at what he's left out, even if it's just to say he says a lot of good things for a Proddy.'"

"Well, if that's his only worry, I'm only too happy for you to fill in the bits missing at home."

"Yes, but it's not just that."

"I know. You're going to say you have to have faith taught at school as well. We've had this conversation before. You can't teach people to believe in God. You have to find Him yourself."

"Of course, you're right; but if you're in school, you learn other things, too—like how to behave, right from wrong, morality—and my father thinks that can be done properly only by God-fearing Catholics, I'm afraid. And I have to say, I can understand his point of view."

"And my father doesn't want his life ruled by a parish priest. He's his own man—under God's providence, of course, but nevertheless . . . I don't think I want to be ruled by a parish priest either." Fred slouched over and put his face in his hands. "This is getting us nowhere. We're arguing now. I just can't see what we're going to do. Are they seriously saying that we can never see each other again? My father is so desperate for that to happen, he's sending me off to the States! I suppose, at least, he realized I'd have to go that far away to get over you."

"You could go, you know."

Fred looked up at her, incredulous.

"I could what?"

"Go."

Fred thought back to the moment he had told his parents.

His mother cried as if someone had died. She wept bitter tears as she looked over to her husband. It was hard to determine whether if she had been on her own, she would have come around; but the sheer, unforgiving stance of her husband dominated. He had remained silent, the look, first, of mistrust and then horror, as Fred confessed his feelings, was overwhelming. He did not speak for minutes that seemed to Fred to last for hours. When he did finally say something, it was in a voice so quiet, Fred had to strain to hear it.

"Never." And then he left the room and the farm. And that was it. The "never" meant that they could not discuss it again, never broach the subject in any way, shape, or form.

"But that would mean admitting they're right, and I would never see you again," he cried, bringing himself back to the present.

"Not if I came, too."

"What?"

"Not if I came, too. I mean, I couldn't come with you now; but if I saved and you saved, eventually, we'd have the money for another ticket."

"I knew there was a reason I wanted to marry a clever woman," he said, springing to his feet, pulling her with him. "You are a genius. We can't tell them, of course."

"Not at first, but I would have to tell them in the end."

"But they may still stop you." Fred looked anxious again.

"That's a risk I'm prepared to take."

"Well, if you're absolutely sure. We can tell Hilda, of course. She can be our go-between. I'll write to you there. And I'll send you an address when I have one."

"Hasn't your father already got you a lodging? Can't I write there?"

"I think you'd better not. It's someone connected to the church, and you don't know. They may wonder who I'm getting all these letters from."

"I'll just ask Hilda to post my letters inside hers."

"I'll look like I have a very devoted sister!" Fred finally laughed.

"Don't worry. We'll find a way."

The end came too soon—far, far too soon. They met on the lane where they had walked all those months ago, but now, the joy they had felt was replaced with sorrow, the laughter with tears.

"Don't cry," Fred urged. "We'll write, and the time will go quickly. It will. I promise, it will."

She didn't stop crying, of course, as he folded her up in his arms.

"Come on now," he said, trying to soothe her but with a choke now in his voice, too. "Come on. It'll be all right. I'll sell men's clothes for a year, and you'll be over before you know it."

He took her by the shoulders and looked at her, his own eyes full. "It'll be all right," he whispered. And then he kissed her one last time before breaking away and wiping her tears once more.

"You keep this for your walk home, in case you need it," he said, handing her a crumpled handkerchief. Then he turned and left, as if he had to get away or else he wouldn't go. He lingered a moment, his hand across his eyes, and then he was gone.

PEOPLE SAID YOU GLOWED WHEN you were pregnant, but she had never seen as much as a glimmer, let alone a glow, in her mother. The curse, as it was often called, didn't seem as much of a curse when it was replaced by a parasite growing inside you. A woman's body did not seem to belong to her through most of her adult life with the constant threat of children, even death, hanging over her.

They frequently talked about some aspect of it in the suffragist meetings.

"It's so unfair," Lotte said. They were discussing a charitable committee that provided help for the women whose lives had been altered, in some cases irretrievably, by conceiving out of wedlock. "Men get to 'sow their seed,' yet it's the women who have to pay!"

"Yes, so unfair," chimed in Ann. "And, of course, they blame Eve."

"Everybody blames Eve," agreed Elspeth. "She seduced Adam and so set off the whole chain of events. But Adam agreed. If he hadn't been so stupid, it might have been different. Eve was dealing with the devil. You can understand her being deceived, but Adam had only to say, 'Who did you hear that from?' But no. He was flattered. So typical of a man! And yet Eve—and every woman after her—has all the pain and suffering, and the men never have to face the consequences, never have to take the blame. It takes two people to make a baby!"

"Yes, there's never anything about 'we both got carried away.'"

"Or worse, the poor girl was forced against her will. And still, she is the one left carrying the baby. Literally. And there's none of the spirit of forgiveness we're meant to believe in either."

They all sat deflated.

As if to rouse their spirits, Hilda said, "I visited that children's home." But she added, "It was such a bleak place. There wasn't much love in it—none really. The children were all so regimented. It was like I was an inspector. They all had to stand behind their beds while I was taken 'round by an awful woman, who kept talking of the shame that these children had been born into and how it was her civic duty to help. She was saying it in front of the children, and they must have understood what she was saying. It isn't their fault, either, but she seemed intent on their knowing the sins of the parents . . . It was all just 'civic duty.'"

"Not all children end up in a home, though. I have heard of families where the baby has been brought up as an afterthought of the parents, the mother becoming a kind of sister," Ann commented, trying to brighten the conversation. "Of course, some couples do marry; but then, you often get marriages where the couple live apart in everything except the marriage certificate."

"I'm sure that's the case with the Murrays." Hilda laughed, in spite of herself. "But that's not the point," she added once again becoming more serious. "Some women do the most dreadful things just to avoid having a child. They have scalding hot baths and drink gin or stick knitting needles inside to stop being pregnant. It's awful, just dreadful." She shuddered. "But the consequences are so infinitely worse for some women than they are for a man, they're prepared to do anything to stop it. It doesn't bear thinking about. And you're right—it's always women who get the blame."

"It is the shame of it that's so awful," said Niamh. "Mothers are meant to see the condition they're in as almost a marker of shame. There are convents dedicated to taking unmarried mothers—which, on the surface, seems like a good thing, but from what I hear, they don't treat the girls well at all. They think they have grievously sinned and no amount of Hail Marys are going to relinquish the consequence they are bearing inside them. Then the baby is whisked away, and the poor girl has to live on with the shame of it all, like a kind of curse."

"So, being accepted into a convent is almost like a punishment in and of itself," Ann said.

"Well, of course, it shouldn't be," Niamh replied. "But I can see why you might think so."

"So, which do you think is worse—the crushing weight of the Church, all penance, and little forgiveness or the burning wrath of God, forgiveness preached but none practiced in reality?" questioned Hilda. "Honestly, the women on the committee I went to were so cold and indifferent, they were almost hostile. You should have heard them; they were relentless in their questioning and absolutely lacked charity in every sense. If anything, the women were harsher than the men. I honestly think they looked down upon the victims—because that's what they were—asking, no begging, for help. Sometimes, I despair. So much for emancipating women if the women themselves are worse than the men. I was intending to help, but the conversations that went on after they left … They were just dreadful, saying, 'They might be looking for food and clothes now, but they should have thought about that before they became pregnant!'"

Yet Hilda's indifference, almost reluctance, to having children had changed. It had crept up on her slowly. She hadn't spoken of it to anyone at first, certainly not her fellow suffragists. She felt almost embarrassed that anyone fighting for the emancipation of women would yearn for anything so conventional as motherhood. But she did.

And then Elspeth told the group that she was expecting, and everyone seemed genuinely pleased.

"I might not be able to go to Belfast and hear Margaret Cousins, but having a child is not going to stop me fighting for the cause."

"I should hope not," said Ann. "You may not be able to help destitute women either, but you can still write letters. And who knows? You may have a girl, and then that'll be another person to fight for women's votes."

During the meeting, Hilda had joined in the enthusiasm of the group. But afterward, she confessed to herself her own desire to have a child. She decided to ask Elspeth over for tea to discuss it.

They had just sat down, Hilda having poured her a cup, when everything she had harbored over the last few months burst forth, cascading out of her in ways that she later thought were overly to the point, given that Elspeth was expecting.

"You aren't worried about your own health?" she asked Elspeth. "I am so pleased for you, but seeing my mother offsets some of my wish to have a child. I know it sounds ridiculous, but however much I want one—and I do—I am worried. I'm worried about morning sickness, the fatigue, and—I don't want to say it, given that you are pregnant—but some people don't survive!" Hilda paused and looked anxiously at Elspeth's pale face, where the only color about it came from her numerous freckles.

"Of course, I'm concerned. How can I not be?" she replied. "But I think some kind of maternal instinct took over, and broodiness got the better of me. Besides which, I hope that William will support me, unlike other men."

"I'm so glad you said that! I long to have children. It's just that I'm a morass of contradictions! I haven't spoken to anyone about it at all—not even Charles, really—and I speak to him about everything! You see, I'm also worried that I may not even be able to have children, and that, in some ways, is worse." She stopped again. "I'm so sorry just telling you all this, but you're the only woman I know who's a suffragist expecting a child!"

"Don't apologize. I understand. I do. I don't think there is a woman who doesn't. But I suppose the need to have children outweighs all other considerations, even though the consequences—as you so rightly point out—can be fatal. I suppose, in the end, we all assume—or have to in our stronger moments—that it won't be us. I still get anxious, though. I mean, I am carrying another life. It's a shame you don't feel you can talk to your mother, but it's important you speak to Charles."

"I will; I will. He is nothing like my father, and I know he'll help if I ever do manage to conceive and be sympathetic if I don't. But I can't tell my mother that the reason I'm worried is because I look at her and think I don't want to end up like her."

"But you do want to end up like me." Elspeth laughed.

"I confess I do—almost in spite of myself."

It was only a few days later that she spoke to Charles. She hadn't planned it at all. She was scrubbing potatoes in the sink, crying over them, depressed that she had started that morning with the same relentless regularity with which it always occurred.

The wretched curse, she thought. *Now, it's become a curse because I don't seem able to conceive, rather than the pain just of being a woman.* She picked up another potato. And then Charles arrived home early and saw her dripping tears into the water.

"What on earth is the matter?" he asked. So, she told him. "Why, on earth, didn't you tell me before? I hate to think of you worrying away at something without letting me know—especially something as important as this."

"I know. I know. But you seemed happy enough, and . . . I don't know. I thought that maybe that was enough, but now, I know I do want children."

"And so do I, but I am fine if I don't have them either. Who knows? Maybe it's just God's way of testing us in some way like Sarah or Hannah in the Bible."

"I don't know what kind of test it is," Hilda started, sniffling back the tears. "It might be that we're meant to be looking after Stuart and Henry at the moment, giving my mother some relief."

"Absolutely."

"You know, in an odd way, looking after them so much, despite their ebullience, was what finally made me want children."

"I love having them around. All the boys against you!" he joked. "Seriously, though, it's grand—even though they can be so naughty and get themselves into so much trouble, I love the way they seem to clutter up the house. It's almost as if we have adopted them already."

"When they were first born, I think I was more of a mother to them than my own was." She stopped and thought for a minute. "I suppose the pattern has just continued. I almost think of them as my own. And yet they aren't, are they?"

Charles hugged her.

"If you want to have children, then we will try more seriously. And if it works, then I will attempt at all possible costs to make it as painless as possible. I will make sure you put your feet up, so you don't get varicose veins and swollen ankles. I'll give you iron to stop you getting tired; and although I don't think there's anything that can stop morning sickness, except perhaps ginger, I will do everything I can to help around the house. I know all the local midwives and will make sure you get the best. Anything else that will allay your worries, they shall be yours. And if you don't conceive and I can't find any more reasons, why, we will officially adopt Stuart and Henry. How about that?"

She kissed him. "Thank you for being so understanding."

"It is as always my pleasure."

So, they had set about it in earnest, and still, nothing happened, which only made Hilda more miserable.

At this same point, the relationship between Fred and Niamh became known, and it was in the turmoil of those few weeks that Hilda conceived. Her mind had become so focused on Fred's leaving and the fact that even if Niamh would see him again, she, Hilda, almost certainly wouldn't. She stopped thinking about conceiving so completely that even when she was late, she didn't stop to consider whether or not she might be expecting a child. Only when he had left and the sadness of the event had fully sunk in did she realize that she had a new life growing inside of her.

Charles believed it was God's gift. "He knows how much you loved your brother, and so He has given you a new life to care about. 'Everything works together for good to them that love God,' as the apostle Paul says."

Even if she thought that was true, she still wished that part of the bargain wasn't one that took Fred across an ocean. He would never see his niece or nephew. He would hear about it in letters, might even be able to see a photograph, but would never hear their voice or see their smile.

It gave her an infinite sense of loss made worse when she received the first letter he sent from America. Hilda sat at the table, upright. Her back was straight, her eyes cast down to the small writing on the sheet as she read the letter again. He had arrived. Her expression started to soften.

He couldn't write that much because it was expensive to send letters across the Atlantic. So, he'd managed to fold the letter in half and then half again to be able to get as much in as he could, and he'd written it in small handwriting, too. At times, that made it hard to decipher, but it was all so well-intentioned, and the letter was just for her. Another letter to her parents and the rest of their family was on its way.

Much of the letter was straightforward. He told of the journey—first to Liverpool and then on the Baltic—and finally, how he had arrived in Philadelphia. He wrote as he talked—frank, open.

> Well, I am finally here in the United States, where they claim everything is bigger and better. It's certainly bigger, but I have yet to see if it's better!

Only in the last paragraph did he get into the subject Hilda had been dreading—Niamh. She could feel the ache he was experiencing from three thousand miles away.

> When you see her, please, please, tell her I am working hard to earn enough for her ticket. I know you can't kiss her, but hug her and tell her that I love her as much as I ever did. Please, please, tell her.

She put the letter down. He was bereft of anyone dear to him, and he was so far away. She felt the pull of his longing, the dull sense of his missing home—of his missing her, of his missing Niamh. Of course, she would hug Niamh, and of course, she would tell her how much he wanted her there with him, that he was saving every penny he earned in the shop to pay for a ticket to America. But that certainty was also so hard for her to bear because she, his own sister, would never see him again.

FOR NIAMH, WAITING FOR FRED'S first letter to come was agony. Niamh struggled even further because she had no address to which she could post a letter. She had been waiting desperately to hear something, but nothing had come.

It had been almost a month since he had gone—twenty-seven long days. "Patience on a monument smiling at grief"—wasn't that what Shakespeare had said? Only, she wasn't either patient or smiling, and every day, she had become more agitated, less patient, and less smiling.

Her family attributed her silence to Fred's parting. They didn't know that the relationship continued, and yet without a letter, Niamh was almost persuaded that it had finished on that evening. The only memento left was the handkerchief Fred had given her on that last day and the memory of his kiss goodbye.

She curled up on her bed, lifted the crumpled handkerchief to her nose, and inhaled deeply. She knew it didn't smell of him anymore—never really did—but it was the only thing she had left of him. She could remember, as if it had happened only a moment before, what he'd said when he wiped away her tears with it.

Her thoughts came back to the present with a jolt. She felt that crippling pain of enforced separation and the endless worry that Fred would not write and that the postman would never deliver a letter from the States; and that last look and the crumpled handkerchief would be all that was left of him.

And then one came, addressed just to her at Hilda's house.

Hilda gave it to her. "I don't know why it came later than mine. If you look at the stamp on the letter, he wrote to you almost the day he got there. I am so sorry."

Niamh held the letter in her hand. Fred had touched the paper; his hand had written on it; his voice was contained within. Tears filled her eyes.

"Now, don't be going soft on me." Hilda laughed, clutching her rounded belly. "Oh, and I have to give you a huge hug from Fred. He told me to in his letter, so I am hugging you now because I was instructed to, not because you are about to cry," she said, tugging her sympathetically toward her.

"Thank you," Niamh said, wiping away a tear. "It's just the relief of hearing from him. A month is such a very long time. I know he wouldn't abandon me, but it's the waiting, the endless waiting. It's all been too much."

Hilda touched her arm with affection. "I know. It's been hard enough for me; it must have been just terrible for you. I have to go out and meet Charles; so, you sit here while I make you a tea, and then I'll leave you alone to read the letter."

After Hilda left, Niamh sat down on the kitchen chair and placed the letter on the table in front of her. Her heart melted as she read the opening.

Dearest Niamh,

I long for you to be here, to hear your voice, to listen to your conversation, to hold you tight and feel your breath upon my face.

Niamh felt a tear trickle down her cheek. *Fred.*

But if I write like this and think of you—touching you, lifting those dark curls out of your eyes and kissing you—I cannot cope at all. So, know that when I write of other things, it is all a distraction until you are here. I will describe where I live and who I have met—all of which are deflections from the agony I live with every day.

Niamh tried to stop crying, but she couldn't. She choked on the tears; her shoulders heaved with the sobs that gripped her. Minutes passed before she could return to the letter. As he had promised, the tone changed, and there was a hint of optimism.

He talked of what he was reading on his lunch break—*Huckleberry Finn*—and then he went on to describe where he lived. It was on a long road, the houses large and varied. Some had a porch; others had steps up to the entrance; some had a portico, while others still had a plain front door that opened straight onto the street. All were different and so much grander than he was used to—or, at least, they appeared grander if size was what you were measuring. He pointed out they were not as impressive as some of the enormous houses you found scattered around at home in Ireland but went on to say that those were the homes of the gentry. These house, the ones in Philadelphia, were of the middle classes, and the area was recently built and expanding.

Of course, he added, there were parts where the houses were bigger than those in the small village of Toombe Bridge. Belfast had large houses and was growing fast, too, but it was the space that the houses occupied, the scale—the fact that they were all different in their own way. It put their mark on the neighborhood as if they, also, were part of a newfound gentry. He couldn't help but be impressed. Each must have its own architectural plan built according to what the owners wanted.

In Belfast, the streets, even those with detached houses, tended to be all the same. Whole areas marked out on a map produced houses that were built to the same specification, size, and type indicated the class and the buying power of the owner. Here they were individualized, and the background of the purchaser was less clearly delineated.

Niamh tried to picture the city of Philadelphia as Fred was seeing it—bigger, better, brighter—but she struggled, even more so as the letter ended.

> *You know how I feel about my da, so I am not excusing him in any way. But I am grateful to him for setting me up in lodgings with the Irwins. They have that forward-looking mentality that is so common in America.*
>
> *When I first arrived, George Irwin shook my hand and said, "Even if you start with nothing, you can always do something with your life. This is your chance to start again."*
>
> *And that's true. Here, your life isn't shaped by your past, by your beliefs, by who you once were and would forever be. That's the difference. Our parents live in a present that is dominated by the*

past, looking to a future that history has already written. But we
can start again, unencumbered by anything.

That was Fred. Robbed of everything he wanted by his father and sent thousands of miles away, and yet still, he could turn it around and find something to be glad about, something to look forward to. She longed to have that spirit, but the melancholy of the situation overwhelmed her, and her eyes filled with tears once more.

"Penny for your thoughts," said Erin, who had just come into the staff room. "You seem miles away."

On the other side of the ocean, thought Niamh, *in faraway Philadelphia.* She stirred herself and turned. "I was just thinking of the near-riot I started with my fourth years. I thought I'd try out a Protestant way of thinking about Cromwell, and Nuala almost punched me. She said— and I quote—'How can you say that, Miss O'Conner? Killing any of them was wrong. They deserved to be free, not oppressed by some Puritan from over the water.'"

Erin looked horrified. "And she was absolutely right to say so. I knew I liked that girl. What on earth made you do that? Put the Protestant point of view. Haven't we got enough of their lies? Honestly, Niamh. Saying he might have had a point in decimating the Catholics. That's outrageous."

"So it was pointed out to me by Nuala. She was very clear."

"That's what you get for thinking like the other side. Shame on you," Erin added, half good-humoredly, but with a warning note.

"Seriously, though," Erin continued, "how will those children know that we need Home Rule if they've had all that Protestant clap trap given to them? What will you say next? That James I was right sending all his Scottish friends to laud it over the Catholics? And what about the Battle of the Boyne? The Irish peasants defeated by an organized army. It's all wrong. Those English won't understand that we're a nation ruled from overseas by a Parliament that knows nothing about us unless we make it abundantly clear. They were happy to let us starve to death fifty years ago. Food enough for the Proddies but none for the Catholics."

Niamh was silent. She recalled a conversation with Fred about the Potato Famine.

"You know, we went as hungry as the Catholics," he said. "There were Protestants who weren't deemed fit enough to feed."

"That's nonsense."

"It's true. When my grandparents were children, they almost starved to death. The government in England helped only those who were of the Church of Ireland. The Brethren got nothing."

She had been surprised, so she had looked into it for herself and found there was an element of truth in what he said.

"You spend far too much time with that suffragist group," Erin admonished. "They're all Protestant, aren't they? I warned you not to attend those meetings."

"It's not them. Really, it isn't," Niamh said. "It's just that my subject can be so divisive and, in our case, sectarian. You know, there can be completely different ways of looking at the same event."

"Yes—the right way and the wrong way," Erin chimed in firmly.

Niamh laughed. "Just because I put Oliver Cromwell's point of view doesn't mean I don't hate him just as much as you, but if you're going to study history, you have to look at how the Protestants might think before crushing them with the weight of the Catholic argument."

"It's a pity the Orangemen don't see the Battle of the Boyne in that balanced way," Erin replied sarcastically. "I don't know how you teach history. Stick to math. That's my advice. Facts. The Protestants can't tell me that two and two don't make four."

"Well, exams set by the British help. I can always pass off the blame to them."

"I would definitely do that. Changing the subject—I hope completely—what have you got this afternoon?"

"Sweet, little first years and nothing that I will get lynched for. It's 1066 and William the Conqueror."

"Ah, the last time those islands were invaded by someone from across the sea. That's the trouble with the English—always conquerors, never the conquered until we get our freedom! Make sure you point that out to your first years," she said, gathering her books for the afternoon session.

"I will. Don't worry."

Niamh gazed out across her classroom. In front of her sat twenty-five first year girls. It was the last lesson of the day, and she could tell she had lost the concentration of all but the most eager. The keenest were sitting in the middle, anxious to catch every word she said. One of them, Bridget, had that questioning look that went with someone who loved the subject and wanted to know more. Her pale face, violet-blue eyes, and black hair made her look as if she were a personal advert for the Celtic nation. She was not one to be typecast, though, in any passive role. She was a pupil who was determined to be her own self.

Just like me, Niamh thought.

She dismissed the class, reminding them to learn the dates of Edward the Confessor's death and the various contestants for his throne, including the two Harolds and William.

As she walked home, the full force of her problem struck her again. She was in love with an Ulster Scot, his family sent over in the Plantation. Hundreds of Presbyterian families were sent over to Ireland by James I to settle there and bring a bit of Protestant enlightenment to a savage country ruled by Catholics. That was what she would have to teach next week to those same fourth years. How could she have a balanced point of view? James I was wrong, and yet, the Plantation had produced Fred. She felt exhausted by it all.

As she sat down after dinner that evening with some books she had to mark, she opened one and then stared at it, pen in hand, not taking in anything she was reading.

"Had a tiring day at work?" her father asked. "Those naughty girls giving you a difficult time?"

"No." She smiled. "They're fine."

"Something's wrong, though."

"It's nothing."

"It must be something. Tell me. It's not Sister Bernadette, is it? She can be a bit of a tyrant."

"No, it's nothing like that."

"Well, what is it, then?" He started to look concerned.

"I think it's my subject."

"Your subject? There's nothing wrong with history." And he was off, actually lecturing, but in that disarming, almost lyrical manner that made you want to listen to him. "It's our culture, our heritage. Without knowing our history, we wouldn't be anywhere. And our legends are everything. Think of Fionn Mac Cumhaill and his son Oisin, who married your namesake, Nismh Cinn Oir, and lived in the magical isle of Tir na Nog."

"Legends are one thing," Niamh interrupted before he went on too long. "History is quite another. It would be easy to teach children about the fairies and the leprechauns. It's quite another to teach them about the English Civil War." She hesitated slightly. "You see, I have a feeling that if we were English, we'd take a very different view of the roundheads and cavaliers."

"You're talking about Cromwell, aren't you?" He spoke abruptly. "He was a monstrous man, who killed countless numbers of our Catholic men, all so Ireland could remain attached to England. I'll not have you defending him in this household."

"Of course, I'm not defending him," she exclaimed. "But if I were English, I might quite like him for being a rebel and cutting off the king's head." She paused, waiting for her father to jump in.

"I can't believe you're putting up the Englishman's point of view. Is that what university did for you?" He seemed both horrified and upset.

"No, they didn't teach me to think like an Englishman, but they did encourage us to think of both sides. And you approve of that, don't you? You often say to the pupils in your school, 'Think of it from their point of view.' Surely, it's a good thing to do."

"Well, that's a maybe. But defending Cromwell? That's anathema."

"He's not particularly well-liked in England either, precisely because he cut off the king's head. He turned England into a republic, and that goes down very badly with those people who loved Queen Victoria and now Edward.

"But I'm certain that those people in the English Parliament who support Home Rule are secretly roundhead sympathizers or would have been if they'd been alive then. I mean, Wolfe Tone was a Protestant, don't forget, and he was one of the greatest fighters for Irish independence ever. It's as if we've forgotten that. We're so caught up in our religious divide, we can't seem to separate our faith from our principles and our politics."

"Well, I can tell you one thing," her father commented. "That university did a very good job on your argumentative skills. You seem to have given this a lot of thought." He looked at her. "And you're sure that this is only an intellectual challenge?" he asked as he pressed her arm affectionately.

She leaned back in despair and, avoiding the implication of his comment, replied, "I don't know. It just seems that everything I want to teach has such monumental repercussions. You're on one side or the other. Look at your man Yeats. He's absolutely committed to Irish independence, and yet because he's Protestant, do we think he's not Irish enough? It all seems so atavistic." She looked down at the exercise book in front of her. "Do you think it will ever change?"

"I don't think it will change any time soon. Home Rule is too big a question."

"That's the thing, though, isn't it? It even gets in the way of considerations that should be above it—like women getting the vote. Erin won't join me in fighting for women's suffrage because she thinks that we have to get Home Rule first. And if I disagree, you'd think I'd betrayed the whole of Ireland. She's so intransigent, so dogmatic. And usually, I really like her. I would say she was my closest friend; yet we simply can't agree, and it's started to cause tension. Why can't it be both? Why must we be culturally divided even on that?"

"Now, there, I can agree with you."

"At last, we have some common ground!" She laughed. "I hate arguing with you."

"That wasn't an argument. That was a civilized disagreement, and to use my own dictum, I can see your point of view. But we're living through difficult times, and sometimes, it will seem impossible. You're teaching something that has been a battleground between our two communities for at least three hundred years, if not more, and you can't solve it. History isn't neutral. And with those wise words, you have some marking to do, and so do I."

Afterward, lying in bed, her two younger sisters sleeping in the bed beside her, Niamh thought of the day that had just been and the conversations she'd had. She wondered how they would have gone with Fred, even Hilda. She smiled. Fred would have agreed with everything she'd said.

"You're the one with the degree. What can I add?" he would have said. It seemed so easy with him. All that visceral hatred between the two communities seemed to disappear. He'd even given in on the baptism of children because it mattered so much to her.

"I don't think baptizing a child before they can even speak does anything for their immortal soul," he had said when they had discussed it. "For me, you get baptized as an adult, and you're fully immersed. It's like dying with Christ and then rising with Him. Seeing someone baptized is really quite a moving experience. But if you think a child is damned to hell if they're not christened at birth, then we'll baptize them all. It won't make any difference to their salvation, and I'm sure God will understand."

She missed him dreadfully, with a kind of ache. Tears welled up in her eyes, and she wiped them away. It was all just too hard. She thought about Hilda. There was something so forthright about her, and she'd encouraged them, too, determined to show that Catholics and Protestants could unite. She liked Hilda and thought her genuine; but maybe it was easier to appear gracious if you were on the winning side, and then, like a nervous tic, Niamh thought the opposite. The Protestants were terrified of losing control. Back and forth, endlessly to-ing and fro-ing. She was just so tired of it all.

Oh, Fred, she thought. *Where are you when I need you the most?*

8

THE IRWINS, WITH WHOM FRED lodged, had been careful around him. They knew some of the background as to why he had come to the States. The elder in the church at home must have told them something, and he was sure his father had, too. Maybe not everything, Fred suspected, but enough to make them sympathetic when he first arrived.

No one back home—or, at least, not the people he knew—were ever that open about what they felt, and to ask too many questions would definitely be seen as prying. So, he was never asked about Niamh, never asked about how he was holding up; and when he had first arrived, they had tolerated his long silences and his wish to be left alone.

One day, he overheard Dorothy Irwin telling her husband, "Leave him be. He'll come around in the end. We shouldn't push anything on him for now. Ross said something about his being involved with some unsuitable girl. That's why he was sent to America. We have to give him time to get over her."

"Maybe we should take him to some of the sites, show him a bit of American history. Settle him in that way."

"Don't go lecturing him, though. I know what you can be like. Here's Independence Hall. Here's the Liberty Bell. This is where they signed the Constitution."

"All right. All right. I won't. Though it's hard not to, as this is where it actually happened."

Dorothy laughed. "I know; I know. And they had an idea for a brand-new country, away from the persecution of the past."

"Exactly."

"Looking to the future instead of being mired in the past," she went on, a hint of irony in her voice.

"Don't mock America, Dorothy. It's a nation built on hope and opportunity. And the sooner we can get Fred to see that, the better. He's only a young man, and if he's anything like his father, he'll have a bit of the entrepreneur about him."

So, the Irwins took him to Independence Hall to see the Liberty Bell and on a day trip to Valley Forge.

"This is where Washington hunkered down in a bitterly cold winter," said George, being slightly more of a college professor than Dorothy wished. "And they nearly died. In fact, many of them did. But Washington held on, and everyone around him was saying it was a mistake and that he was bound to be defeated because they had just lost Philadelphia. There's a famous painting of Washington kneeling in the snow, praying for the army's salvation."

Dorothy interrupted him before he could carry on. "Yes, but in the late spring and early summer, it's a lovely place to just come out of the city and walk."

"And it's a very good place to remember that even if things seem grim at first, a little perseverance and forward-thinking wins out in the end," added George, not wanting the opportunity for a message to be lost.

Niamh would love to come here, Fred thought. *A new republic being formed by defeating the British.* He wrote to her all about it in his next letter.

> *You'll love it when you come. It's very anti-British, and you don't have to be a Catholic to think that way. Even the Irwins, who are very Ulster Scot in so many ways, have truly become American citizens. It's as if they have forgotten all the religious and political tensions they left behind—as if they were part of the old country, to use an American expression. They're interested only in what the future holds.*

Now, Fred supposed that some of the Irwins' efforts had slowly been rewarded. He was less overwhelmingly sad than he had been at the beginning. He wouldn't call it depression, but everything around him had been gray—as if the whole place was covered in such a thick mound of dust that he couldn't shake it off. But slowly, the carpets were beaten and the surfaces polished so that now he had begun to see America for what it could be.

The Irwins had been surprisingly gentle with him about churchgoing, as well. They had started to mention it only after about a month into his stay.

Dorothy broached the subject first. "Why don't you come to our church on Lombard Street?"

George was not one to leave a history lesson untaught. "You know, it used to be called the Central Colored Church. One of the founders of the Underground Railroad was an elder there."

Fred deferred. "I'll just read my Bible, if you don't mind."

"Are you sure?" George persisted. "The Underground Railroad helped slaves escape from the South. Some of the people in the church were actually born slaves. It's extraordinary that they abolished it only fifty years ago and that those plantation owners thought it was perfectly all right for them to have slaves and treat them like animals. The church campaigns for former slaves to be heard."

While still not wanting to attend the church, Fred was, nevertheless, interested enough in it that he included it in his next letter to Niamh.

She wrote back:

> It's strange, isn't it? Although I know it's actually not the same, many Catholic tenants on those huge estates owned by the Anglo-Irish feel that they are as good as slaves. They have no freedom, live in grinding poverty, and some of them starve to death. And yet, if the Irwins lived back home, there is no way they would approve of Home Rule. I suppose I should be glad that in America, they can embrace the rights of the downtrodden and oppressed.

It was these letters from Niamh that encouraged him the most. He could hear her voice through the written page; and she became less a person living on the other side of an ocean, so far away that the thought of her could be captured only fleetingly in letters, and more of a person, with whom he was going to meet up again, share all those experiences in the present, and begin to understand what changes of attitude living in America could bring.

Perhaps that was why he had first thought about going back to church. There were plenty of churches near where he lived in West Philadelphia, but he hadn't been to any of them, hadn't been near a church at all since he came to the States almost four months ago.

He felt he was done with God if religion was the thing keeping him apart from Niamh. But now, it seemed that God had faith that the two of them could be together.

With this in mind, Fred found himself entering the Tenth Presbyterian Church just off Rittenhouse Square. He had been strolling along the sidewalk (as he was learning to call the pavements) one lunch break, exploring the city by himself, when he came across Rittenhouse Square. It was about only five minutes from the store, but for some reason, he hadn't gone that way before.

But now, here he was, sitting alone at the back of the church, one among possibly two, if not three, thousand worshippers at the end of July. It was so different from the small assembly he had gone to at home. It was built on a grand scale and had a church spire that seemed to want to reach right up to the heavens. All the lines inside were clean, the pulpit and the space around it open, the galleries tidy under rounded arches.

He looked around at the congregation, dressed up in their Sunday best. Then Rev. Marcus A. Brownson started to preach. He read a passage from Joel 2, and Fred deliberately stopped listening, disgruntled at the thought of another tirade from the God of the Old Testament. Distracting himself for what he thought was going to be the inevitable fire and brimstone, he thought of Niamh.

"You can be far too serious sometimes," he remembered her saying as she had kissed him on his cheek. "You have to learn to laugh at yourself." He smiled. He was beginning to smile more as he dreamed of their future together.

Suddenly, the minister's voice cut through his meandering thoughts and appeared to address him directly.

"Here's what He's saying to you," Rev. Brownson said. And Fred, somewhat taken aback, sat up and listened. "It's time to take an opportunity of grace—either time to turn or return to the Lord. It may be a time when you've backslidden, and God's got you in here and to this point, where He's saying, 'Return to the Lord.' Maybe you've thrown away your Christian faith, and the Word is saying, 'Return to the Lord.' God has a way of speaking to you through His words."

Fred was electrified. He knew that the minister could not actually be talking to him alone in a congregation of thousands, but it seemed to apply so directly to him. He hadn't been to church in such a long time. Maybe he had thrown away his Christian faith; maybe he had been backsliding; maybe it was God, using Rev. Brownson to say, "Return to the Lord."

The minister went on. "The trumpets are meant to awake you to eternity. This life is not all there is. We're not bound to time. God, in His great love and mercy, sends these words to the world."

This was so different from the sermons on the Old Testament he was used to hearing. The God of the Brethren seemed to be an angry and judgmental God, not a God of goodness and grace and forgiveness. Fred was transfixed.

"He's blowing a trumpet," Brownson continued. And then he added as an aside, "Trumpets were often used to signal the coming of the prophet . . . to blow a trumpet in your ear to awaken you so that He might say to you, 'Turn to the Lord; trust in the Lord; call upon the name of the Lord and you will be saved.' God is gracious and merciful, and this is a day of grace."

The sermon ended, and they sang the last hymn, "Amazing Grace." It was such a well-known hymn, but now he listened to it with a new fervor, the message of the sermon having resolutely struck him. He could call upon the name of the Lord and be saved. The God of Tenth Presbyterian was gracious and merciful, not the tub-thumping one of the Brethren that made Him sound so terrible that you quaked at the very thought of Him. This was a day when the Grace of God could save—to use John Newton's words—"a wretch like [him]."

The church started to empty, but still, he remained where he was sitting, his head in his hands.

"Can I help you at all?"

Fred looked up. It was Marcus Brownson himself, walking back through the church to his study.

"That was a powerful sermon. It's strange, but I felt you were speaking just to me."

"God often has that effect. Is there something I can help you with?"

"It's all right. I was just leaving." He hesitated. "You don't often hear sermons like that from the Old Testament."

"What do you mean? I often preach from the Old Testament in that way."

"I mean, saying that God is merciful and gracious. Usually, you hear a much grimmer version of God."

"The God of the Old Testament is the same God of the New."

"I suppose I'm not used to hearing it put like that. My father is a preacher, of sorts, and he would never give a sermon like that."

"How does he characterize God, then?"

Fred thought hard. "Well, it's difficult to say."

"Try," Rev. Brownson encouraged.

"I think that although he believes that God saves sinners, there isn't much joy in it. You made it sound like there was a fanfare every time a sinner was saved—you know, blowing trumpets. My father's faith is a very dour affair."

Rev. Brownson sat down beside him. "I hope you don't mind my saying," he said, "but you don't seem to like your father that much."

It was the same directness that he had once relied on from Hilda. He laughed. "I can see you have had this kind of conversation before."

"Not this exact one, but ones that are similar. So, why don't you like him?"

"It's a long story."

"I have all the time in the world." And it seemed to Fred in that moment that he did—something about the way he sat comfortably in the pew looking kindly at him but with an authority that made him want to talk.

Fred sighed. "It's about a girl."

"One of those stories, then. Let's hear it." Rev. Brownson leaned back into the pew, ready to listen intently.

"She's a Catholic," Fred began, and the whole story started to unravel—the months of silence and tension that he had endured. It all came pouring out—a great, long rambling of everything that he had thought and felt over the past four months.

"Well, that's some tale you have to tell, and some things you need to say to the great Almighty, too," Rev. Brownson said when Fred had finally stopped talking and sat staring at the floor. "What you have to remember is that He is a God of love, and He understands everything, including your love of Niamh. But He would want you to forgive your father, too. From what you say, he does care about you. He knew that this was a serious relationship, which is why he sent you here. But he can't be happy about it. For him, it's like losing a child."

"It isn't as if I died," Fred said with feeling.

"Have you lost a brother or sister?"

"How can you tell?"

Rev. Brownson rested his hand on Fred's arm. "You might not have actually died, but for him, it's as if you *have*. It's as if he has had to sacrifice his relationship with you because in his mind, marrying a Catholic is a grievous sin and because he will never see you again."

"But it isn't a grievous sin. You just said that God is loving, but my father thinks He is vengeful. He was so angry when I told him about Niamh. Besides, I write to them regularly."

"I know, but just be him for a moment. How would you feel if all you want is for your son to know God, and he's done the one thing that will stop him from doing that?"

"But he's wrong!"

"He may well be, but he doesn't think so. And that means that, of course, he's angry. But that doesn't mean you have to be angry, too. You need to forgive him as God forgives us."

Fred looked up as Rev. Brownson continued. "I've found that when we actually forgive someone, it has a beneficial effect on us, as well as being the right thing to do. I'll give you another example from the Old Testament, if I may."

Fred nodded.

"It's not a perfect analogy—and I may have to mix my metaphors a little—but you are a bit like Jonah—and not just because you went to sea." He laughed. "Jonah went to sea because he was avoiding what God wanted him to do."

"I wasn't avoiding God in coming here."

"I said it wasn't a perfect analogy. And your father isn't God either. But you are still running away from both God and your father in lots of ways." Fred shifted uncomfortably in the pew as Rev. Brownson went on. "Let me follow through my point. Jonah realized that he couldn't escape God; so he told the people of Nineveh his message, and they repented while Jonah went and sulked under a tree."

"So, I'm like Jonah, sulking," commented Fred, beginning to be exasperated once more.

"No, no, not sulking," Rev. Brownson replied quickly. "But I think you're angry with your father, and it's getting in the way of you understanding God's grace for what it is. Jonah understood it in the end. He, too, was angry with God because He could forgive the people of Nineveh, even though, to him, they were utterly reprehensible and ungodly in everything that they did. But in the end, he saw that was what made God so wonderful."

"How?"

"Because He could forgive even them."

Fred looked down at his hands as Rev. Brownson sat back again silently in the pew and watched Fred clasp his fingers together.

"Can we ..."

"Of course, we can. Why don't we thank God for all He's done for us and pray, too, that He will give you the strength to forgive your father. There's no bitterness in the hope and joy of the Lord."

9

"SHE'S RIGHT, YOU KNOW," NIAMH said in the staff room one day.

"Who is right?" Erin asked, looking up.

"Jane Austen."

"Right about what?"

"About women who've lost someone they love suffering more than men."

"What made you think of that?"

"Nothing, really. I just re-read the novel *Persuasion*," Niamh lied. She was adopting a new tactic for talking about Fred without actually referring to him. "You haven't read it, have you?"

Erin smiled. "You know me too well to ask that."

"Well, in *Persuasion*, Anne Eliot is talking to this young sailor, Benedict—not Benedict, Benwick—something like that—in Lyme Regis."

"Lyme Regis? Where, even, is Lyme Regis? Honestly, the books you read."

"It's on the south coast of England, I think. Anyway," Niamh went on hurriedly so as not to miss the point she was making, "his fiancée had died, and so they were talking about whether or not men suffered more. Anne said that men got away from home and saw other places, other worlds—particularly if they were sailors—so there was always something which would help distract them. Whereas, women were left at home and had the things around them that were touched by the ones they had loved. They lived in the settings where the relationship had first occurred, so in some ways, they harbored the love they had in a kind of uninterrupted way with nothing that could deflect them."

"I didn't think Jane Austen was meant to be so depressing."

"She's not. It all turns out all right in the end. Anne marries Fred." There was a relief in being able to say his name out loud, even if ostensibly, she was talking about a fictional Fred—Fred Wentworth, not Fred Anderson.

"So, the person she's talking about isn't dead, then."

"No, she is persuaded not to marry him at the beginning by a family friend because he's not rich enough—really, because he's the wrong class. He's a sailor, and she's a minor aristocrat."

"It's not surprising that Benedict disagreed with her, then. He loved someone who had died. The man she loved was still alive, and she was just too snobby to marry him."

"And she bitterly regrets it. Besides," Niamh added, "she would have married him. It's those around her who wouldn't allow it." She hesitated before saying, "It's as if she wanted to marry someone who was a Protestant, someone who was completely unacceptable."

"That's completely different," Erin said, outraged. "Your class and your faith are not the same at all. How can you say that?" She slammed the books she had just picked up down onto the table. "Honestly, Niamh, I worry about you sometimes. The Protestants have taken away everything we have. It's not just unacceptable. It's wrong. All wrong. So much worse than marrying someone who was not quite your class. I mean, if I must, I can see Jane Austen's point of view. But if she lived here, she would never have a Catholic and a Protestant wanting to marry. Why did you say that?"

Niamh, discouraged and dejected, knew now that even displacing what she really felt wouldn't help her discuss the one thing she really wanted to say to her friend—that she had met and fallen in love with a Proddy. It was too great a betrayal of everything Erin stood for, believed almost as passionately as Niamh did about Fred, maybe in some senses more so.

Yet in order to keep up the pretense of talking about Jane Austen, she added tentatively, attempting to focus on what she really wanted to say one last time, "I suppose Jane Austen was saying the relationship rose above those class distinctions." She looked over at Erin, still fulminating. "I suppose she might say, if she were writing about faith, that Protestants and Catholics do believe in the same God!"

"Honestly, Niamh, if it's not history, it's novels," Erin spat back. "I don't think that the Protestants seemingly believing in God has got anything to do with the way they treat Catholics. They have robbed us of our dignity, our homes—even our lives. If you were working class in England, you would probably say that," she muttered but with a sense of defiance. "For such a sensible person, you come out with outrageous views from time to time. It's a wonder I still like you."

"Don't say that. Please, don't say that." Niamh realized she had gone too far. "I was only talking about a novelist who lived nearly a hundred years ago. I wasn't"—she hesitated—"saying that Catholics should marry Protestants."

"I should think not. Where would we be if we had Catholics sympathizing with the Orange Order and the red hand of Ulster? Nowhere! That's where. Absolutely nowhere!"

"I promise you, I will keep all further controversial thoughts to myself."

"You shouldn't even be having them," Erin said angrily.

"I know; I know."

"I keep telling you. It's that women's group. They might be fighting to vote; but they're all Protestant, so they aren't facing the real question, are they? Irish independence. They probably don't even want it."

Niamh looked up at her, her expression apologetic, but she said nothing.

Erin took a deep breath and, losing some of the anger in her voice, said, "It's not that I don't want women to get the vote—of course, I do—but not now. We have to have independence first. And I worry about you. It might be all right for you to say something like, 'Jane Austen thinks that Catholics should marry Protestants' to me."

"I didn't say that," Niamh protested.

"No, but you did draw the parallel. And as I said, you can say something like that to me."

"And get my head bitten off."

"Quite rightly, too. But there are other people around who, if you even hinted at the very idea, would do so much more than bite off your head. Our life doesn't rest in some romantic novel, you know." She rested her hand on Niamh's arm. "You know I'm right. Be careful what you say."

"I'm sorry. I was just trying out an idea with my oldest friend."

"And I still am," Erin said, squeezing her arm and smiling for the first time. She added, "But only just! And on that note, I am going to teach my first years."

It always came back to a bitter sectarianism, and it saddened her. There was no way she could discuss the loss of Fred with one of her oldest friends, not even through a novel, because that bitter divide was about more than a person's faith. It was political. And there was no space for someone to stand in between. You were either Catholic or Protestant. One or the other. Never both.

Niamh looked around the staff room with its tables, stacked with exercise books and comfortable chairs beneath the tall windows. Austen was right, though. She might not have had anything to say about the Irish question, but she did know what it was like to be a woman. Maybe that was another reason that she had gone to that first suffragist meeting. It allowed you to believe in something that didn't tear your country into warring factions and wrench long-standing friendships. It allowed you to unite in a common cause, where your faith was all but irrelevant.

She gathered up her books and thought again about where she had begun the conversation. Austen did know about loss and love, too, even if her own talk with Erin had gone so badly wrong. Niamh was still in Ireland with everything comfortingly familiar and yet forever changed by Fred's absence. Fred. Fred could see their new life because, in a way, he already had it. She did not. He could write with enthusiasm about Philadelphia, a place she had never seen.

Walking along the corridor to her next lesson, though, she thought of his last letter and had to smile.

> *I can just see you walking down the street on my arm, a new hat on your head, gloves up to your elbows, turning heads. It'll be grand.*

"He always tries to include me in his letters. I mean, he paints a picture of Philadelphia and says what we'll do together when I'm there. And I know he's doing it to show what our life will be like together; but I'm not there. And I don't know—it almost makes me feel worse."

Niamh was helping clear up after a suffragist meeting, unburdening her thoughts to an empathetic Hilda. She put the plates and teacups into the sink and started to wash them half-heartedly, her mind not really on the job.

"Do you know he's reading only American authors now, too? He says he wants to immerse himself in what they think. The latest one has an American marrying someone who's lived in Europe so long, he's become European." She scrubbed absentmindedly at a plate before Hilda gently took it from her hands. "He said in the letter that it proves Catholics can marry Protestants as nobody seems to care about that. It's more about the attitude to life, about how Americans and Europeans weigh up their lives and their possessions, but it doesn't seem likely to end well. And it isn't at all clear that Osmond has become a Catholic, anyway."

Hilda continued listening intently, allowing her friend to continue.

"There's an older American woman in it, too, called Madame Merle, which might imply that she did, at least, marry a Catholic Frenchmen, but it isn't ever mentioned. Osmond just likes art, and Isabel Archer is another one of his trophies. And what's worse is she seems to have given up all pretense of freedom in marrying him," Niamh added with an emphasis in her voice which wasn't reflected in the way she looked. She seemed close to tears.

Hilda was about to speak when Niamh exclaimed, "I'm being ridiculous, I know. It was more of an aside when he said that. He isn't saying that Osmond or Madame Merle are good people. I mean, he does know that they're awful, really." She plunged her hands back into the sink.

"Of course, I know what Fred's trying to do. I do," she added with a conviction she didn't appear to feel.

She paused, holding a dripping plate in her hand, while Hilda waited, unsure whether to answer her pronouncements as questions or to just listen and let Niamh's distress run its course.

"But you can't distort everything just to satisfy what you so want to be true," Niamh continued, now going back on what she had just said, her voice rising again. "And he certainly can't hold the book up as an example of a good marriage." She wavered. "Not that he's trying to," she said. "It's just that Catholics can marry Protestants, and no one cares."

She dropped the plate with a splash in a kind of resigned despair. The curtains, hanging limply above the sink, were doused in water. The very air around the women seemed weary.

"Niamh," Hilda began but was interrupted by the continued tirade.

"It seems so churlish of me, and of course, I don't want him to write as if I have no part in his future. But he can see it so clearly, you know?" She seemed increasingly miserable, as if everything, not just washing the dishes, had become a chore that would never end, as if the whole world had become a stubborn mark that she had to scrub at endlessly.

"So, in one letter, he kept talking about the stately villas around where he lived and the parts of the city that were endlessly being rebuilt. Even the store that he's working in is being completely refashioned into a shop, which will eventually be eight stories high. And it's by describing it that he wants me to see it as though I was there."

"For someone who left school at fourteen, that's quite an ambitious task," Hilda said, trying, at last, to lighten the conversation. "And let me clean those plates," she added.

"Sorry. Sorry. I'll concentrate on doing the dishes." Niamh turned her attention back to the sink. After a few moments, however, she stopped again. "You know, he even sent me a postcard of City Hall with a man called William Penn perched on top of the building. I think he is aware that his descriptive powers are somewhat wanting. He may read a lot, but it hasn't helped his powers of description." Finally, she half-smiled, suds dripping off her hands.

"I am glad that he's finding his feet. Of course, I am; and I should be grateful that he imagines me there. In his last letter, he said I would love the place he worked because it was just so full of stuff that I could buy, even ridiculous things like fascinators and gloves. He kept telling me that there was so much variety but that he's saving every penny for me to get there as soon as I can." Niamh sighed.

"And that depresses you?" asked Hilda, listening to Niamh's voice becoming increasingly fragile the more she talked and watching her gaze wistfully out of the window.

 Niamh said nothing at first. She was all too conscious that she was telling Hilda those things which she could no longer explain to Erin, and she suddenly longed for the easy relationship she had shared with her before Fred.

She turned toward Hilda, grateful that she did, at least, have someone with whom she could explain how she felt. "Of course, I want to be there with him. Of course, I want to see him desperately." She smiled again, tears filling her eyes. "It's not that I'm depressed. It's just that everything—my life in Ireland, his in America—is tainted by a kind of melancholy."

Hilda didn't say anything, instead waiting for Niamh to speak again.

"You see, I don't have to describe where I live to Fred," Niamh began. "He's lived here all his life. He knows it—the few lanes that make up Toombe, the river running through the middle. And yet now, it must seem all so far away, almost forgotten. He doesn't hanker after it, you know. His letters never mention the pub in the center of town or the uneven houses next to it on either side. He's never mentioned Toombe Bridge.

"It's all, 'In Philadelphia, they do this or that in Rittenhouse Square, and the streets that surround it are elegant eighteenth-century townhouses.' Or 'the crack at the Irwins was grand.' I mean, he does miss me, of course, but his way of dealing with it is to look to the future, which is good, but it makes my life seem stuck in some ways because I'm not there." She paused. "And in some ways, I feel increasingly separated from him because I love where I live, even the rain."

"I'm sure they have rain in Philadelphia." Hilda laughed, touching Niamh's arm to comfort her.

"Yes, but you know what I mean. It's as if he's forgotten all that beauty—those undulating hills, 'the Emerald Isle'—for some kind of mesmerizing city sprawl."

She looked over at Hilda holding a teacup, dripping in her hand. "I think I miss them for him, and I'm still here. So, I feel sad. I miss him more than I can say." Her voice cracked slightly. Niamh looked down at the plates.

"You don't have confession in your church, do you?" she asked Hilda, suddenly changing the subject. "But, then, you do confess to your priest?"

"Well, we don't even have a priest, of course."

"Yes, but in most Protestant churches, they do, don't they?"

"I suppose so—a minister, at least—but I wouldn't say we confess. Why do you ask?"

"It was Fred's last letter." She wanted desperately for there to be something in common with what they did in church, yearned to find a way that they could speak the same language.

"What did it say?"

"He went to Tenth Presbyterian Church and told the priest there all about us, about the pent-up emotion he had been feeling over the last few months and said it all came pouring out of him. He said he told him everything. He said he didn't mean to, but it all just came out and was such a relief.

"I'm glad he did, really, because he hasn't had anyone he could tell. I mean, I have you, but he doesn't." And she did, she realized, have Hilda and could talk to her in a way she couldn't to Erin, could even speak to her in a way that Fred no longer did. "I understand that Rev. Brownson doesn't know anyone involved, doesn't know me," she continued, "but just telling someone could mean that you gain some perspective on it as well."

"I'm glad you feel you can talk to me."

"Haven't I just proved it?" She handed Hilda another saucer.

"And you think that was like a confession?"

"Well, it is in some ways, isn't it? He is a man of God; they were in a church, and they ended up praying at the end."

"Do you know I don't really even know what you do in Confession?" Hilda's voice was deliberately layered with sarcasm. "Except that we're very much against it," she half-joked.

"I think it's one of the good things about being a Catholic," responded Niamh, seriously, not taking up the jibe.

"Really? Why?" Hilda changed back her tone to one of genuine inquiry.

"Because it's a way of reminding you that you have done things wrong and you have to admit them. It's a way of telling us that we're all sinners. The Confession even begins by saying, 'Bless me, Father, for I have sinned,' and then we list our sins."

"Have you ever told your priest about Fred?"

Niamh rinsed and dried her hands. "I haven't."

"And is that because you don't think it's a sin?"

"Partly that, I suppose." She thought about Father O'Rourke. He was a nice enough man, middle-aged with thinning hair and a hearty laugh. Jovial. That was what he was. It was a good adjective to describe him, yet he had a serious side, too. He was capable of being somber when the bells at Mass were rung, when the bread and the wine actually became the body and blood of Christ. Yet she couldn't imagine telling him anything about Fred.

"And I suppose because I know what he'd say if I did."

"That it was wrong."

"Yes, and also because he'd be speaking with the full force of the one true church behind him." And that one true church was represented on this earth by men, jovial though they might be. "Just out of interest, why do Protestants think Confession is a bad thing? I thought they all wanted sinners to confess."

"We do, but without a priest in between."

"What do you mean?"

"Well, to get theological for a moment," said Hilda, putting down her tea towel, "it's there in your opening words. 'Bless me, Father.' We don't think He can bless you—properly, that is. Only God or Christ can. And then there's absolution, as well. Nobody can say, 'We absolve you,' as the priest says. And you can't do penance for your sins either. Nothing *we* do absolves us of our sins. Only Christ's death does. That really is the heart of Protestantism. It's what Martin Luther realized on the Sancta Scala."

"He had to come in somewhere, didn't he? We were all one church until him. And then, we weren't. He just had to protest." Niamh reflected. "I suppose confessing your sin to a priest makes it less abstract, though—more real, in a way. You are saying it to God—yes, through a man—but to God, really. And the ritual of saying 'Hail Mary' can help. It's like a reinforcement reminding you of what you have done wrong and that you are forgiven."

"It's funny. When I talk to you, I can see what you mean, even if I still don't agree with it. It would be so much better if we could just talk to one another instead of never meeting someone because they support the antichrist." Hilda laughed as she hung the last cup on the dresser and then hugged her. "Thank you for that."

Niamh walked home. It was a beautiful evening, the pungent smell of freshly cut grass in the air. She could hear two boys laughing down the street, clearly headed home after having been down by the river.

"I'm still wet from when you pushed me in. And we didn't even catch any fish. I'll get you tomorrow, don't you worry."

"Not if I can help it."

They ran on past, pushing and shoving each other, joking as they went. She felt that sudden pang again. She longed to be with Fred, of course, but suddenly felt that overwhelming sense of nostalgia, strangely misplaced, for her countryside upbringing—one that, if she lived in Philadelphia, she would no longer have and her children would never experience.

It was safe where she lived, where Fred used to live. But that part of her existence—the walks down meandering country lanes and even, she had to laugh, the smell of manure—was going to be hard to sacrifice. Life in America might not be dogged by the same religious wars that existed in Ireland, divisions that tore one community from another and threatened friendships. But at least, she felt secure when she walked out. America, for all Fred's enthusiasm, appeared like a dark cloud, threatening the hope to which she clung.

10

HILDA WALKED UP THE STREET to her husband's chemist shop. Hanging above the entrance, jutting out, was a sign with his name on it—Bell. It was designed to look like a lantern and was made of glass. In the winter evenings, it was lit up from the inside. Hilda liked to think it had a bell-like shape to match his name, though it tapered at both top and bottom; and she couldn't imagine what bell would actually be shaped like that.

The window had a display in it—potions and pills stacked up in their neat boxes along with glass bottles that contained perfumes. There were soaps, too, in elaborate paper, mounted next to a picture of a cherubic child blowing bubbles. She liked the display. Arranging things in the window had been part of her job, and she had enjoyed it. Now, it was Sarah's role, and she did it well.

She opened the door and a bell clanged her entrance.

Sarah and Albert looked up from behind the counter.

"I'm here to see Charles." Hilda smiled.

"He's out back," Sarah said. "How are you doing?"

"I'm getting along fine. I'm not sick anymore, which is great. I think the middle bit is the time when you're meant to glow. I don't know about that, but I know I'm not that lovely shade of green anymore."

"Oh, don't say! That really puts me off expecting. I don't like feeling even mildly queasy. I can't imagine feeling like that all the time."

"And you don't get used to it either. But it is worth it—or it will be. That's what I tell myself. The strange thing is that once it's stopped, you can't believe it happened. Three months—nearly four—of feeling as sick as a dog, and it wasn't just the mornings either. It was all day. I think it was the worst around five, but now, miraculously, I feel fine."

"Until you get really big and then you can't wait for the labor. That's what my sister tells me, anyway, because otherwise, who would want to give birth?"

"You can go through to see him any time you want," Albert interjected, clearly tiring of a conversation in which he could take no part.

Hilda laughed.

"One day, you'll marry and have to face all this. Well, not you, but your wife, and then you'll just have to listen."

"Not me. She can talk to other women but not me." He shook his head and turned to a customer who had just walked in.

"How can I help you?"

Hilda went through to the room at the back of the shop. Charles was there, carefully measuring and then transferring liquid from one bottle to another with a pipette. He concentrated hard before turning to Hilda to greet her.

"Sorry. I have to be so precise. Too much and I'd be poisoning the patient."

"That's all right. I love watching you practice. It's amazing that you know what substances to mix together. I haven't a clue and would definitely poison the patient!"

"You wouldn't if you knew what you were doing."

"You mean, if I could get my head around all those complicated equations!"

"Yes. And what is more, you could. You've got a pretty decent brain inside of you. Who's the one who organizes all those meetings? It's you. Who's the one who writes all the letters and decides whom to send them to? It's you. I will continue to tell you until the day I die, you've got more get-up-and-go than almost anyone I know, and that includes the men. And I don't think having a baby will make any difference to that. Men, beware. Hilda is on the war path."

She grinned. She was thankful to God that she had found someone who not only loved her but also encouraged her in every way. It would have been so easy for her to have married someone who simply saw her as a wife, or a wife and mother, and who didn't see the woman behind those labels. But Charles saw her as that and more. He saw her potential.

"So, you want me to take more iron. And not just to make me into a fighter."

"Yes. I think your mother was, and still is, really anemic. I've said it before, that's why she looks so tired and washed out all the time. You don't want that. It's really important. And as you don't drink dark ale, I can give you these tablets, and you can get it that way. Here're some for you and also for your mother, too."

"Yes, m'lud. Anything you say. Anyone would think it was you having the baby. Honestly." She stroked his arm.

"I just care about you, that's all. I want everything to go right. I want to protect you."

"I'm doing fine. But if it'll make you happy, I will take the iron tablets, and I'll give some to Ma as well."

They could hear the people in the shop. "And will the lotion definitely stop my hands from chapping?" a woman asked.

"Yes, it will if you apply it first thing in the morning, any time after you wash, and then last thing at night," Albert instructed.

"Because they're really sore at the moment. Look the skin cracked all between the fingers—see?"

"I can assure you it works wonders. My mother swears by it."

"All right then. I'll have some."

"Another sale assured," Hilda whispered to Charles. "Albert does a great job. Does his mother even have dry hands?"

"Less of your cynicism, young miss," said Charles. Kissing her on the cheek, he added, "Now, I must get back to work. You can't distract me anymore."

"Are you sure?" Hilda looked up coquettishly.

"Yes, I am. Absolutely sure. Now, go."

She turned and went through the door, blowing him a kiss as she went.

She was meeting Niamh in half an hour, but first, she had to collect her two wee brothers. She was looking after them again to give her mother—her anemic mother, as Charles had diagnosed her—a break.

It must be wonderful to be able to look at someone and decide what was wrong with them and prescribe them something that would make them better. It was like you saw inside their body—what the blood was doing as it pumped around and, in this case, wasn't pumping sufficiently.

She thought of those strong men lifting weights. They had iron in them, muscles bulging, and her mother could lift only the equivalent of a spoon. She might not be able to tell what was wrong with her physically, but she would fight for what was wrong with her in life. She was glad Charles wanted her to have more vim and vigor, and that was more than just physically, too.

She came to the farmhouse and saw her mother seated on a bench outside. Her pale face almost disappeared into the whitewashed wall behind her as she gazed out in front of her, looking at nothing in particular.

"I was just having a wee sit down before I got on with the cleaning," she explained to Hilda.

"Charles thinks you're anemic."

"And what's that mean?"

"It means your blood lacks iron and makes you feel tired all the time. He's given me some, too. It's what's in the ale they make women drink when they're expecting, but this way, you don't get drunk!"

"And here's me thinking I was weary because there was so much to do."

"Yes, there is, and that's why I've come to take Stuart and Henry—to give you a break. Where are they?"

"I think they're out in the fields at the back. Call them. They love their sister Hilda. They get more attention from you."

She squeezed her mother's hand and walked around the house, calling as she went.

Stuart and Henry tumbled into view with grass-stained trousers and muddy elbows, hair awry.

"Come on, you two. Let's get you cleaned up, and then I'll take you back to my house."

A short time later, both suitably scrubbed and in slightly cleaner clothes, the boys each held onto one of Hilda's hands as she said goodbye to her mother, who was still sitting on the bench, still unmoving.

"Make sure you take those pills, Ma. They may perk you up a bit. You can only try." She leaned down and kissed her. "I'm off, and I'll keep the boys overnight. Remember the pills!" she insisted one last time, and then, two boys in tow, she walked off down the lane.

She held Henry's hand as Stuart went ahead, stopping off along the way, picking blackberries as he went.

"Save some of them for tea, and if you pick enough, I'll make some jam as well." Seeing what Stuart was about to do, Hilda suddenly cried out, "Put them in this basket."

She caught up with him, but she was too late. His clean shirtfront was already smeared with blackberry juice.

"Honestly, Stuart, no sooner have we cleaned up one mess, you create another! What'll we do with you?" She laughed and ruffled his hair. "Come on. Let's pick the best ones without eating them now."

He obeyed, though he did sneak the odd one here and there.

Hilda often wondered at her friendship with Niamh. They had grown closer, particularly over the last few months since Fred's departure. She was, after all, the post office for his letters. But it had begun to develop well before then, since she had realized that Fred was interested in the Catholic girl.

She had often thought about why he had selected Niamh. She was, Hilda supposed, funny and fiercely independent; and she had a kind of authority that meant she could quell a class of rowdy girls. She also had the confidence of someone who was prepared to defy convention, and that was considerable.

That last attribute was more Hilda's own take on Niamh. Niamh was prepared to declare that women were just as good as men and should be treated as such. There was a defiance, a take-it-or-leave-it, in her attitude that was needed if women were going to stand up to men—"be on the war path," as Charles had put it.

On the other hand, why someone like Niamh had fallen for Fred was a mystery. He was loyal, which was a good thing, there when you needed him to be. And she supposed, when she stopped and thought about it, that he was quite good-looking, had that boyish hint of mischief about him.

She looked down at young Stuart. It was the same roguish charm, she thought. But that wouldn't be enough to demand the sacrifices she knew Niamh was making. It might explain the initial attraction but not the kind of devotion that kept you together, even when you were pulled apart—and what was more, meant defying your family, even the Church of Rome. She really admired that determined spirit in her that once she had decided something, really committed, there was no turning back.

Niamh arrived at Hilda's house shortly after Hilda and the boys had returned home.

"Boys, go play while I chat with Niamh," Hilda said to her young brothers.

"So, what's the crack from America?" asked Niamh as soon as the boys had left the room. "Any letters for me?"

"Yes, there are two—one for me and one for you."

"Have you read yours yet? Any news on how the funds are coming?"

"No, not as such. I think he's getting there slowly but surely. I think he's frustrated at how long it's taking." Hilda looked at her oddly. "Surely, he must tell you."

"Yes, but I think he's so anxious for me to be there that he doesn't like to disappoint me. I think he might be more honest with you. He keeps sending me these cheery missives all very enthusiastic about how great it'll be."

Niamh frowned, hesitating before she continued, seeming reluctant to say what she thought. "I know he means well, but there are times—and I hate to say this—when I find his sunny disposition infuriating. He was even talking about forgiving our parents in the last letter I got. Honestly, how can he say that? They're the whole reason we're in this mess to begin with."

"I know. I can find him very irritating, too! I honestly don't think he means to be annoying. I just don't think men know what we want to hear, and he's not around so that you can clip him 'round the ear and tell him not to oppress you with cheeriness. I think that's what he thinks you want to hear. You know, 'it's all very positive here in the States. Nobody cares if you're Catholic or Protestant. We are all citizens of the U.S. of A., and it'll be grand when you are, too.' And he doesn't have anybody telling him that you might want to hear something more."

"He does constantly tell me that he loves me 'to the depth and breadth and height [his] soul can reach,'" Niamh reflected.

"Of course, he does, but it would be good if he gave you a better idea of how long you were going to have to wait before you saw him again and stopped going on about forgiving our fathers!"

"Very, very true," Niamh acknowledged. She shook her head. "I think he doesn't realize that my being a Catholic is so much more than just what I believe. It's part of who I am—my identity. Even if I rejected the whole lot of it and called myself, heaven forbid, an atheist, I would still be a lapsed Catholic. You don't have that phrase—'a lapsed Protestant'—you would just be a non-believer.

"The thing is, I keep having all these complicated wrangles in my head, and I can't tell him because the letters take so long to get there. I know it'll be better in America; they don't have the history, the taboos. But still. I'll always be a Catholic, lapsed or otherwise."

Hilda looked across at her friend sitting hunched over the kitchen table, her hands threaded through her hair. She thought of her Charles. There were no quarrels or arguments as to what they believed. It was so much simpler. They were on the same side in everything.

"Yes, but don't forget he fell in love with you, *knowing* you were a Catholic, and it didn't make a difference. I'm not a Catholic, and I think you have become my closest friend."

Niamh looked up and smiled.

"Yes, but we've got other things in common. We're both women, to start with. Long live women's suffrage. But there are so many Catholic women who think Home Rule is more important. Honestly, if my friend Erin knew she would be as difficult as my father . . . She thinks the Protestants keep down the Catholics in the same way as you and I think that men rule over women. And there's a whole history that says she's right, as well." She sighed. "I'm sorry to say all this to you. I've just been sitting on it for so long."

"Don't worry. I'm always here." She rested her hand on Niamh's shoulder. "And remember, Fred doesn't have anyone he can talk to, as well as the fact that he's a man. I'll leave it up to you to forgive your father, but you might forgive Fred for being Fred."

Niamh got up and hugged Hilda. "I better get going, or the people at home will wonder where I am." She took the letter and left.

Hilda called the two boys in from the garden. "All right. Who's going to help me squash these blackberries and make some jam?"

11

"There's enough carpentry work to keep me going for years, right enough. Well, possibly not years, but long enough. Thanks very much for letting me know," Niall said.

"I've never seen anything like it," he continued. "Well, I mean, I have in New York, but still. And even after they've finished the building, there's all the joinery for the interior. It's just amazing. Do you know that in the middle of the building, there'll be nothing at all, just a load of galleries all looking into the middle? So, when you're shopping for your suit, you can look up and think, *Those are mighty fine cushions. I'll take me a couple of those, and while you're about it, the wife would look very pretty in that dress.* That John Wanamaker is a clever man."

Fred laughed. It was so good to have Niall here in person as opposed to in New York He had missed that day-to-day friendship they'd had on the boat, the amiable banter of the man from the north of Ireland. Niall's sunny, unaffected temperament cheered him. Fred had discovered that there were jobs available in the new building Wanamaker was building right next door to where the old one, the one he still worked in, stood; so he wrote to Niall to tell him. Fred knew Niall had plenty of work in New York, but he decided that if there was one relationship he could have in person, he would try for it and trusted that Niall would feel the same way. And he had.

As Niall had pointed out on the boat, there was plenty going on in Manhattan and also where he lived in Brooklyn. If Philadelphia was tearing down old buildings to build new ones, New York was doing it even more and building them high. Niall had even described one building in his letters called the Flatiron Building. He said it was like someone had squashed one side of a box but left it standing. It was twenty-two stories high. Everything in New York was up, not out. For a country that boasted of the space it had, New York didn't seem to experience it.

That was another reason why Fred had hoped against hope that Niall would want to move. He had told Fred he was living in a bedsit in Brooklyn and had to share the room he was in with three other men. The bathroom was down the corridor, and the six rooms on that landing, all with people in them—sometimes large families—shared it.

Through the summer months, it had been stiflingly hot. At night, they had opened the window, but that meant the bugs got in and bit you, quite apart from the fleas and the bedbugs. Niall had said he was used to sleeping with others—hadn't even had a bathroom at home—but Fred could tell that he didn't enjoy the closed-in feeling of Brooklyn, the tenements all around with little space to look out and see the sky. Niall was used to the countryside, the green undulating hills of the Antrim coast, the smell of the sea and the waves.

It was true, the Atlantic crashed in on New York—it was a port, after all—but it was a very different sea to the one off the Antrim coast with ancient legends attached, engrained into you from birth like the Giant's Causeway. He felt a knot in his stomach, a churning, every time Niall referred to his home in Portrush, but the friendship he offered was irreplaceable. Although having Niall around brought back memories of the life he once had with Niamh, he was from back home, talked about Ireland with an air of nostalgia in a way that the Irwins did not, and, more than that, he was a Catholic.

Fred turned to Niall, pushing away thoughts of that day on the North Antrim coast, the day he had first told Niamh that he loved her and that she loved him, her Cú Chulainn.

"I'm glad it's working out all right," said Fred. "Glad, too, of the company. I mean, the people I stay with are nice enough, and the folks in the shop are perfectly civil; but it's good to have the crack now and again. I've spent most of my free time wandering around the city on my own. It's nice enough, but you can get a bit bogged down in your own company."

"Always willing to oblige."

"How's where you're living working out?"

"It's grand, right enough. It's clean, and there's more space. Honestly, that John Wanamaker is something else. There he is, building this new, enormous department store; and he houses half his workers in a hostel—the Young Men's Christian Association. He has his hand in so many pies!"

"I think the YMCA is meant to be a charity or something. I think he gives it money."

"Well, it seems that his name is all over it. Why don't you live there, too? You could have your letters addressed there, which would be much easier."

"True, but the system we've got works all right, and I think it's slightly cheaper where I live. I've got to save every penny I can get."

"Still pining for Niamh?" Niall turned to look closer at his friend. "There's got to be a better way of getting money than selling other people's shirts. How much longer is it going to take you?"

"Well, I've been here for sixth months and, at this rate, at least another three years, but she's worth it."

"She better be. Can I get you another pint?"

Niall got up and went over to the bar. It seemed that in every city on the East Coast, there was an Irish bar—not quite like he was used to, in fact, though he had rarely gone into the pub in Toombe. It was somewhat frowned upon by the Brethren Assembly, but here, he could enjoy it. The owners had tried to capture the atmosphere of the pub, but everything was too new. They didn't have the old settles or benches, and even though they'd tried to recreate that spit-and-sawdust feel, it was still a bar, not a pub, still part of the new century unencumbered by the past.

Fred stood behind a counter in the Grand Depot. It was vast—more like an overly elaborate warehouse, a grand market space, built under numerous chandeliers. High above were the skylights that let in additional light. The counters fanned out concentrically, separated by long, wide walkways with slightly narrower aisles between them.

Right in the middle was a tent, where women could see the latest fashion designs and ballroom dresses actually modeled for them. Customers could wander through buying anything from linen sheets to an evening suit for men, guided only by large posters high up above telling them what was for sale in the particular section they were looking. Even in this store, you could glance across and suddenly think, *I've just remembered, I need some new laces for my boots* when out buying some gloves, and you needed only to look up to find out where to go. As Niall had said, Wanamaker was a clever man.

There were advertisements all over town recommending the latest fashions that had just arrived, and people flocked to the store. He rather supposed that they ended up buying things they didn't actually need, but the attraction of the store made it all seem enticing and ever so necessary.

He turned to a customer who was waiting.

"I want to buy a cravat for my husband. Have you any in particular that you would recommend?"

"Certainly, madam. I deal more with shirts, but there are several designs that might interest you." He turned and crossed the aisle, walking along to the next counter, which had a display of silk cravats at the end. "Can I interest you in any of these?"

While she dithered as to which one to pick, he added, "I think these go splendidly with the shirt over here, which is on sale."

She left the shop with two shirts and three cravats. Fred had to laugh to himself.

"You've got the blarney," Niall had told him one evening. "That soft, Irish brogue and the 'lost, little boy' look that has them all convinced that they must buy that shirt and tie. It's not only that Wanamaker had the idea of making a shop that has everything, but he's also employed the people to sell the idea, as well!"

Fred smiled at the thought of the conversation He looked across the store at a woman, struggling with bags and two small boys.

"Why can't I buy the hoop?" one of them was crying.

"If I've told you once, I've told you a thousand times, we are not buying anything for you today. You have toys at home that you can play with, and that'll have to do."

"Yes, but this hoop has a stick to roll it down the path, and I don't have one of those."

"I said no."

The woman looked fraught. Fred interrupted, bending down. The boys reminded him of Stuart and Henry.

"How would you like a gobstopper? But you can have one only if you stop asking your mother for a hoop."

The boy stopped whining and looked up at him.

"Now, your mother knows what you might like for your birthday or Christmas but not today." Fred looked over his head at the mother, who was nodding appreciatively. He handed over a gobstopper to the crying boy, who had now calmed, and one to the other boy, too.

"Yes, I do, and make sure you say thank you to the nice man."

"Now, off you go—and no more complaining."

"Thank you very much indeed. You saved me," whispered the mother as she wended her way off through the aisles.

"Trust you to have a bag of sweets in your pocket." The shop assistant stood beside him, laughing.

"It keeps them here longer if they don't have children squabbling. More time to buy," Fred said with a hint of irony.

"Listen to you. You are becoming quite the salesman."

Fred laughed. "No, I just know how to keep small boys happy."

"So, how do you feel about putting that entrepreneurial spirit to an even bigger test and getting a lot of money fast?" Niall asked later on that evening.

"I keep saying it's not salesmanship. I'm just being nice."

"Of course, you are! All right, then, not entrepreneurialism, but still a way to make a quick buck to get your Niamh over by Christmas. Well, maybe not Christmas but soon after. I have the perfect plan." Niall leaned forward conspiratorially. "Some of the men were talking today about gold and silver mines out West, and people are making a fortune." Niall seemed genuinely excited by the prospect, could barely rein in his enthusiasm.

"I thought the Gold Rush was over. Cleared out California ages ago," replied Fred with an air of caution.

"Yes, but there are silver mines, too, and not in California but further north in Idaho and Washington. We wouldn't have to stay long. Just make our money, and then the world, as they say, is our oyster." Niall's natural exuberance was infectious.

"It is tempting. Very, very tempting. Being a shop assistant is fine, but it really isn't that exciting."

"Exactly! And just think how exciting mining for gold would be— or silver!" Niall pressed on.

"Let's not get carried away," Fred said, punching Niall in the arm. "I'll give it some serious consideration. Just out of interest, how would we get there?"

"Well, that's a bit of a problem, but only a small one, really. You would have to spend the money you've saved so far on a train ticket."

"I see. So, I spend the money I actually have in the hope that at some point, I can get some more. That doesn't seem that promising."

"I can see your point of view," Niall acknowledged, "but just think of the rewards. All that money for you to have. Maybe you could start up a shop like Wanamaker's," he added jokingly.

"I don't think that should be your selling point when I've just said it was dull! How long do I have to think this over? When are you thinking of going?"

"Well, the lads were talking of going in just a couple of weeks. Apparently, it can get really cold and snowy out there, so by the end of the month at the absolute latest—but probably before. Just think of those spectacular mountains! Apparently, the scenery is stunning—just awe-inspiring—and as I was saying, you can get all the way there by train."

"That doesn't give me that much time." Fred frowned. "All right, I will think about it. I promise. So, no more about how great it will be. Tell me more about the shop you're building. I gather they're thinking of putting an enormous organ into that hall they're putting in the middle of the store. What on earth do they want to do that for?"

As he went home later that evening, he started to consider Niall's proposal. It was true he had been wearying of his job at the Grand Depot. It was hard to remain enthusiastic about the array of customers he had day in and day out, asking for items he could see wouldn't fit them or suit them either, but still remaining cheerful because the customer was, apparently, always right.

It might have been better if you actually got to know the customers, but there were so many, he hardly saw the same person twice. Back home in Ireland, you could build a rapport with customers you saw regularly, but here, it was different. There was the occasional person who came in often, like the woman who was always wanting new handkerchiefs to match with whatever new tie she had bought for her husband. You could exchange pleasantries. But that was a rarity.

He got off the train and slowly walked along the road to his house. If he could really earn enough money to buy Niamh a ticket and have something else besides, that would be tremendous. That was providing Niall was right about the claims you could get out there.

He looked down the suburban street with its pretty, Victorian villas stretched in a straight line in front of him. It was pleasant living in Philadelphia, better now that Niall was here and better, too, because he had become more involved in Tenth Presbyterian.

What kind of church would they have out there in the Wild West? And yet, it sounded as if Niall was going to go, anyway, and he would be alone again, left selling men's shirts forever—or so it seemed—scrimping and saving until he had enough money to buy a ticket. And when would that be?

The thought of Niamh overcame him. It was almost unbearable to not see her for so long. And who knew? Maybe she would tire of waiting. Some other dashing man would come and sweep her off her feet. After all, the engagement had never been made public and was broken almost as soon as it was made from everyone's point of view except their own. He was asking a great deal. Maybe too much.

He stopped outside the house on the stone steps leading up to the front door. He would write her a letter explaining his decision and pray that she would agree. Climbing the steps, he resolved to find out, tomorrow, exactly how much it would cost to get to Idaho.

NIAMH CAREFULLY FOLDED THE LETTER and looked up in thought. She knew she should be excited, euphoric even, but the anxiety as to how Fred was going to get the money gnawed at her in a way that she could not shake. It was true, he would potentially be able to earn enough money to mean she could leave by next spring, earlier if his enthusiasm was anything to go by. But mining? Mining was dangerous. She knew that much.

Gold was different. Gold could be found in rivers, and people panned for it, trying to separate out nuggets of gold from the silt found at the bottom of the water. They had found it in Wicklow in the last century, and people had become rich. But silver mining sounded different. It sounded as if you had to dig your way to find it; and if you had to dig under the earth, the whole thing could collapse on you, and you could be trapped with no way out.

The thought of being trapped in an underground mine was a nightmare for Niamh; engulfed in dust and rubble, shut in with no air to breathe and no sky to see—just darkness. It was too unbearable. And then there were explosions that could happen deep down in the bowels of the mine. You could lie dying, and there would be no way you could get to the surface and be helped. Men injured, all without hope. It was terrible, all too terrible. And this was how Fred was going to make his money. He, it appeared, did not have an ounce of claustrophobia about him. It was all positive and cheerful, optimistic.

Just think, we could be together in just a few months. We won't have to wait years, anymore. No more selling shirts or ties. No more having to cram people into suits that don't fit and telling them they look grand. Soon, we will have enough money to buy you a ticket and have money to spare!

There was nothing at all about the conditions he would have to work in. Nothing about how he would live up there, in the mountains, through the harsh, snow-ridden winter. She had been so anxious, she had decided to look up the Rockies in an *Encyclopedia Britannica* in the school library.

She went there after school and entered the now-silent room, taking down the large, somewhat dusty volume and looking up the mountain range. She now sat between the stacked bookshelves, in the fading light of the day, and read what it would be like in the Rockies at that time of year. It was grim. Not only was the winter extreme, but there were also wild animals that could eat you. There were bears and wolves and mountain lions that could polish you off in one fell swoop.

It wasn't as if Niamh didn't enjoy the haunting beauty of nature; she infinitely preferred the gentle, rolling countryside around where she lived to the city. If she woke up early enough, she would lie in bed and listen to the dawn chorus and try and identify the various bird songs. Her father was something of an ornithologist and had transferred his enthusiasm to his children. She liked identifying them—the chaffinch from the goldfinch, the blue tit from the great tit, the family of crows, from a magpie to a raven. It was something she had shared with Fred on their walks out; and once, when they had gone to the Giant's Causeway, they had spotted a sea eagle, flying high above the cliffs, coasting on the air, wings spread out, majestic. But Fred was going to a nature untamed. What was it that Tennyson had called it? "Nature red in tooth and claw."

She noted, as she read on, that eagles were common way up in the Rockies, soaring, thousands of feet high over the vast landscape. Down on the ground, though, you had to be wary, and it was on the ground that Fred was going to be—under it, in fact. The terrain of the Rockies was so very different from the hills of Ireland. The cost of earning the kind of money that Fred spoke of might be too great.

She supposed there were towns near the mines, but they weren't substantial, not like Philadelphia. He had a secure position in Philadelphia—a job, a place to stay. She had gotten used to his telling her anecdotes about the day, about the customers, and about Niall, who had joined him from New York.

She didn't blame Niall for telling him about the opportunities out West. If he hadn't heard it from him, he would have picked it up from somebody else and probably been as keen to go. He seemed to have embraced the American spirit, the rags-to-riches stories of Horatio Alger.

But those stories were sedate in comparison to Jack London, whom he had also read before Niall had even suggested going West to mine. Jack London, it appeared, had been a gold prospector in Klondike in the Yukon, which was even further north than Fred intended to go, and he'd written a novel about his experiences— *The Call of the Wild*. Niamh had tried to get ahold of it but hadn't managed. Reading the same books was a way of bonding with him, experiencing something that he was experiencing, too. The book was full of grueling adventure, according to Fred; but the main character, a dog—which she thought was odd in and of itself—triumphs in the end over adversity. Fred, though, was full of its praises.

At the time, he had been safe in Philadelphia, an assistant in a store, so she had liked the passion with which he described the wild scenery, almost shared his enthusiasm. But now that he was actually going there, she knew she felt differently. She felt an irreconcilable tension—the gripping fear of what he might encounter—possibly was encountering at this very moment—and the overwhelming desire to see him again, have him safe in her arms. That was what she should concentrate on—meeting him again, having him hold her, being able to run her fingers through that tousled hair of his—just the reassurance of his presence once again.

She closed the book and put it back on the shelf, sighing as she did so. It was all too much. She had nearly blurted out the whole sorry tale to Erin just an hour before.

She was sitting in the staff room after the day had ended. Her attention had been miles away across an ocean when Erin interrupted her.

"You look very worried about something. Can I help?"

"No, it's nothing really. I just have a lot of work to do."

"We're going to have to put a stop to your dedication. Between work and that suffragist lot, we hardly see anything of you anymore. I thought I'd see more of you over the summer, but you were always at Hilda's campaigning for this or that right for women. I know it's important, but really, you need a break. Let me take you out. There's a dance at my church on Friday. If you make yourself look as good as I know you can, you might get a dance—and that's a sure way to distract anyone."

Erin meant well. Her kind friendship was so well-intentioned, but Niamh just snapped at her—told her she didn't have time for dances, that they were a frivolous way of making women dependent on men, looking coy and yet flirtatious until they were asked for a dance.

She regretted it the moment she said it and was about to tell Erin the real reason, announce that she was engaged already, when she realized that she couldn't—and that was almost as bad, perhaps worse.

"Well, if that's the way you feel about it, remind me never to ask you again," Erin replied, looking hurt. Niamh was only able to say that she was sorry, that she hadn't really meant it, but that she had a lot on her mind.

"I can listen, you know," Erin replied, somewhat curtly.

But Niamh couldn't tell her oldest friend what her problem was because she knew that she would not accept that she had fallen in love with the enemy—because that was how Erin viewed all Protestants. She knew, of course, that they may be reasonable in and of themselves; but until Home Rule was granted, they were all very much on the opposite side, stopping the thing that was even more important to her than the rights she had as a woman. And all of that was interconnected with her identity as a Catholic.

The conversation ended too abruptly.

"Well, if I can't do anything to make you cheerful because, heaven forbid, it would infringe your sensibilities, and you're not going to tell me what the matter really is, then I am just going to give up and go home."

"Honestly, Erin, I am so sorry. I just can't explain. It's got nothing to do with you." That was only partially true. Her anxiety, her all-engulfing problem, had nothing to do with her, but her inability to say anything had everything to do with what Erin held dear.

Sitting now, alone in the library, she could feel herself starting to cry, tears welling up in her eyes. If she gave into them, she would never stop. She took a deep breath and then another, put the folded letter away, and tried to decide how she would reply. But reply to where?

Their system of writing to the store no longer worked. She was going to have to wait until he arrived, somewhere in the middle of those wretched Rocky Mountains, before she could say anything; and by then, it would be too late. He would have already embarked on this ludicrous enterprise, and she had no chance to say, "Don't go." Why hadn't he asked her before he had gone? Why had he risked everything on just a chance that he would succeed?

She realized what she was doing—letting anger take the place of fear. She knew why he had done it. She remembered Hilda's words, "You might forgive Fred for being Fred," and she smiled. The impulsive, boyish enthusiasm that believed all would go right with the world, the reason that she loved him in the first place, was the reason he had gone to America believing that she would follow. And that was the reason he had gone to the West, too, because he trusted— no, passionately believed—that she would be there so much sooner.

Her smile wavered as the tears came back. Anger was definitely a better way of avoiding crying than love. "Well," she said to herself, trying to be positive as Fred would have her be, "soon, I won't be able to look the Rockies up in an encyclopedia. I will see them for myself."

She got up and walked out of the library, out into the paneled hallway, through the doors, and into the early autumn air, down the drive to the gates of the school. Turning back, she looked up at the large, white building behind her, built so girls like her could study. She gave half a thought to what she was sacrificing by going to America—her family (that was clear) but also, maybe, a small fraction of her independence. Suddenly, it was all becoming very real.

"Sacrifice your independence? Honestly. You? The most independent woman I know. Never. Well, I mean you do have to learn to compromise—that's true—but not lose who you are, who you want to be. And don't worry. I have trained Fred very well. You can't be having second thoughts after all this time? Surely?"

Niamh sat in Hilda's kitchen, holding a cup of tea. Stuart and Henry played outside in the garden.

"No, I am not. Really, I'm not. It's just that the thought of leaving all this has a sudden clarity that it didn't have before." She shook her head as she confessed. "And though I could cheerfully be rid of the majority of my family, I won't have them around anymore, not even to argue with. I won't know anyone out there. I won't have you to put Fred's point of view. I won't have you."

"Yes, but you'll have the actual Fred, and that's the point. None of these letters anymore—just Fred in flesh and blood—and that has to be worth it."

"It is. I know it is. It's just that I won't know anyone there. And who knows? They might treat women even worse there than they do here. Fred won't shackle me, I'm sure; but everyone else might, and I won't know where the suffragists are!" She laughed but expressed hesitation at the same time.

"I am absolutely certain that in the 'land of the free,' there will be someone arguing that women should have the vote," Hilda replied with encouragement.

"I don't know. All those books Fred keeps reading are so very male to me. And one of them is about a dog. I can't even think of a woman writer. I suppose there's *Little Women*, and I suppose Jo wants her liberty."

"Exactly. And there are some more I'm sure, even if I can't think of one at the moment. The thought that there is no one fighting for women's rights is ridiculous. It's more the thought of what you'll be leaving behind than any real worries about what you are going to find when you get there."

Niamh had to admit this part was true. Ireland, for all its flaws—and there were many—seemed so much more tangible than, for now, the ungraspable United States of America. That vast continent seemed so untouchable, it disappeared as she thought of it. The promise Fred offered—which to him was so solid, so concrete—dispersed for her like vapor. Yet, as Hilda pointed out, Fred would be there. She had to stop thinking about going to America, that ill-defined concept, and start thinking about going to Fred. Fred would be there to welcome her and would be her home, not some strange, forbidding town on the West Coast.

She had not shared with Hilda her anxiety about where Fred was going. She didn't know how much Fred had told her, and she wasn't about to be the one to make her as nervous as she was. Hilda was expecting a child, and she knew that in the later stages, an expectant mother shouldn't have anything that made her anxious. These worries she would have to keep to herself; the rest, she argued, were the natural fears of anyone making such an enormous journey.

In this role, Hilda was fighting for her brother, and that was fine. If Niamh told her that he was going down a mine to get the money for her to go, she was sure Hilda would react as she had done. As she never mentioned going West or the silver mine, Niamh could only assume that he hadn't told her, which said something for Fred, too. Maybe he didn't want to worry his sister.

However, the fact that he had withheld information from Hilda only increased her fear. At some level or other, he must have realized that it was dangerous and that he shouldn't say how he was getting the money. She looked out of the window at the two boys playing a kind of tig, though it seemed that they didn't mind being caught as it involved tumbling and mock fighting when they did.

"You're going to have to stop having them around soon. You're getting too large to chase after them."

"I think I can cope. My mother certainly did. And by the time she had those two, she was considerably older than I am now." Hilda put down her tea cup and stared across at Niamh. "You haven't talked about how he thinks he can afford to buy you a ticket so soon."

"Oh, he's ever the optimist. I suspect he thinks he will make a fortune selling men's suits."

"I know," Hilda said. "And I know you must be worried out of your mind. So, I am here to tell you, courtesy of Fred, why you mustn't be."

Niamh broke down. "I am sorry. I know you shouldn't be stressed, and here I am sobbing in front of you. But I am terrified." She gasped and, placing both hands on the table, cried again. "It's just that I see him buried hundreds of feet underground, trapped, and I can't stop."

Hilda bent over her. "It's all right. Fred thought you might react like this, so I am here to provide all the solace you need in his absence and to tell you he'll be fine."

"Thank you," Niamh replied as tears coursed down her face. "Thank you."

13

"HE'S TURNING INTO YOUR FATHER, and he's got you as a spokesperson. He's even said he can forgive him for sending him away," Charles said as he cleared away the dishes from the evening meal. "Honestly, going to mine for silver, so he can get the money faster. What is he thinking? And you seven months pregnant, not wanting to get anxious about anything, have to worry about your brother going down some mine. And not only that, but his only concern is what Niamh will think and not you. He does know you're expecting a baby, doesn't he?"

He put the dishes down rather too firmly in the kitchen sink, and they clattered loudly as he turned on the taps.

"Let me do that," said Hilda, laughing as she pushed Charles aside. "You'll break all the crockery." She added soap to the water. "I'll let you dry the dishes if you are very, very careful."

"Seriously, though," Charles replied, picking up a plate with exaggerated caution, which made Hilda smile. "It is a bit much. You're supposed to calm Niamh down when you must be anxious yourself. I'm all for the dour Ulster Scots buttoning down on what you actually feel, but aren't you at all worried? Or does your family all share a business ethic with little consideration of risk?" He turned and put the plate up on the dresser behind him.

"Of course, I am worried, but I know Fred so much better in some ways than Niamh. Or, at least, that side of him. It's not that he's reckless, and at least this time, he realizes that someone might think he's being foolhardy. It's more that he's always looking for opportunities to make good and to improve things in some way so that even if the situation seems awful, he will look forward and see how eventually it will be better." She paused, still holding a dish in her hand.

"I remember when Martha died. He was quite young at the time. Although he was devastated, he still wasn't defeated by the whole thing. My mother just withdrew, and my father became so stern, always quoting the Bible at us—and the gloomier parts of it, as well—but Fred, in a way, kept going. He wasn't going to be broken by the experience, even though he was so terribly sad. He helped me survive it. Of that, I'm sure." She looked up at him as he took the plate from her hand to dry it.

"Maybe." Charles looked down at his wife, still concerned.

"I think that's one of the reasons that he can look at our father differently. He doesn't hold a grudge—well, not forever. He tries to see the good in people. That's why he fell in love with Niamh. The fact that she was a Catholic was irrelevant. She was a good person, and so he loved her."

"I can see that," Charles replied but went on, turning the issue back and forth in his mind, nearly wiping away the pattern of the plate as he thought. "The thing is, despite all the bigotry between Protestants and Catholics, it's an easier thing to say Niamh is a good person than that your father is a reasonable man. That's a very hard thing to do. And he does have a tendency to pick those sections of the Bible which most suit his point of view."

"He most certainly does, and my mother, in particular, has suffered from it," she said with feeling. "But I have to say that for all I cannot bear his views on so much, the book of Job helped him through that whole period with Martha's death."

"Now you're being like Fred, seeing the good in him!"

Hilda laughed. "No, I'm not. He has treated my mother appallingly, and it's almost impossible to forgive him for that. And I don't like the way he packed Fred off to America without really consulting anyone, apart from the elders in the church. But I do think, like Fred, there is no point in remaining bitter about it for the rest of your life; and one way of doing that is to look at the glimmers of good in my father, however few and far between they might be. Quite apart from the fact that we are meant to forgive those who despitefully use us. I don't think God wants us to hold on to the wrongs people have done against us. So, as I said, Fred looks for the good where and when he can."

"I think, in the case of your father, they may be only the faintest of traces of redemption. And on that note, you should be going upstairs and resting. I will follow you up later."

Hilda kissed Charles and climbed the stairs. She may have said to Niamh that she did not mind having Stuart and Henry around all the time, but she was increasingly aware her movements were getting heavier, more cumbersome. She could feel the child inside of her moving. It was odd. It always sprang into life when she decided to rest, as if her lack of movement was a signal for the baby to become energetic.

She paused on the stairs to feel the baby kicking. Sometimes, when she undressed, she could see the feet trying to break out from under the skin, punching through. She placed her hand on her stomach. "Not long yet. Only two months. Don't be so eager to get out."

Slowly, she began mounting the stairs again. Not that Fred could have known, but the fact that she was expecting a child had turned her focus elsewhere. It was not that she was not worried about what he was going to do, but now, her attention was split between concern for her younger brother and perhaps a greater anxiety that everything would be all right with the birth. If he was grappling with what nature might bring from the outside—the storms, the snow, the rocks—she was worried about what nature would bring her from within—the pain, the blood, the labor.

She knew she was at the turning point. A few weeks more and she would be so large that she would think of nothing else but giving birth, and that it would be a relief. But now, the child was big enough to make its presence very much known but small enough that she could still feel that she was keeping it safe from everything. Yet it was hard, sometimes, to believe that the thing wriggling and dancing inside her, even as she now got undressed to go to bed, really was a baby. And if it was hard for her, it must be even more difficult for Charles. Perhaps it looked like she was just getting fatter.

She smiled. He didn't think she was putting on weight for no reason, of course. Sometimes, when the baby was particularly restive, she told him to feel it kicking. Her nightdress was cotton, and it was easy to feel it through the fabric, the elbows out and feet kicking, the whole of her belly undulating as the child attempted to turn. Charles loved feeling the new life, as yet unseen, but present. His touch was as tender and gentle as if he were actually holding the newborn in his arms.

But there was something different about carrying the child yourself, she thought. You could never forget that growing within you was another life. She knew Charles was not neglectful, would always put her needs first, and yet she also knew there were long periods in the day when he didn't think about their unborn child. He would be lost in his accounts or making sure he had measured out accurate doses of laudanum, even joking with Sarah and Albert; the baby would not be at the forefront of his mind as it was with her. She was not only worried about her own health but the child's, too.

She lay down on the bed, the baby moving within. Outside disease could take it before it ever had a chance to thrive, and the baby was due in December, when winter was approaching its coldest—not, she had to admit, as cold as where Fred would be now, but cold, nevertheless, and damp—the damp that got right into your bones. It was important to keep an infant swaddled against that winter chill. She knew of countless children who didn't see their first birthday. It was remarkable, really, that in her family, they had lost only one child; and she had, at that, lived until she was seven. Yet seven was far too young to die. Only now did she begin to feel what her mother must have felt—the terrible yearning for a child that she had brought into the world living longer than she did.

She lay on her back, hands resting on the moving infant within, and wondered if this was what people called the maternal instinct, that unconditional love for something you hadn't even seen but only felt. Her mind wondered again as it were wont to do. Lying still, apparently resting, meaning to rest, was not easy for Hilda to do. Her mind was always racing from one thing to another: Fred, the baby, its well-being, her well-being, her mother, her father, Stuart and Henry, and then back again. And then there were the bigger things—the rights of women. She paused. There was too much to think about.

Hilda knew that Charles insisted on her going up early to bed because she would be off her feet and resting her body, but, she thought, it really didn't rest her mind at all. With nothing else to occupy her, her thoughts turned into musings, which all too often became wrapped up in convoluted, even tortuous, ideas. Occasionally, she would turn to the Bible and read. At the moment, she would constantly turn to the section where Mary visited Elizabeth: "The babe leaped in her womb." That got her thinking, too, though. Was it that John recognized Mary, even though he was not yet born? Or was it that he was responding to Elizabeth's pleasure, that the mother and baby were one?

She had asked Charles what he thought, and he had just shrugged and said, "Probably both."

Her mind turned again. In her work with women, she had come across those who had tried to end their pregnancy. Awful ways they had attempted to get rid of the baby included sticking knitting needles up into the womb, so desperate were they to stop the life growing inside of them. Sometimes, they hemorrhaged and bled to death, but so anxious were these women, they tried, nevertheless.

The few meetings that she had organized were held in secret; the penalty for aborting an unborn child was a harsh prison sentence. She knew, too, that some considered it murder. The ones who were chosen to hear these women's pleas were very carefully selected. No one she knew could condone it, yet it was so understandable, your heart went out to them. It was passages like the one in the Gospel that made people in the church, both Protestant and Catholic, so against it. The infant, however small, was a human being, one who could recognize Jesus Christ from within His mother's womb.

Hilda felt her child move again. It was true; it did seem to have a life of its own. She noticed the way it responded to music being played, moved with a greater energy when hymns were being sung in church. Yet it was also a part of her.

She had looked in the Bible for guidance when she had first met a woman who had, remarkably in some ways, successfully ended her pregnancy but who was now destitute. There were verses in the Old Testament, some pointing one way, others the opposite. So, David wrote in a psalm that he had danced before he was born. But in Leviticus, God's rules said that if a woman was killed by robbers, they should be put to death; but if she lost a child at the time of the attack but she survived, they should be punished only as thieves.

She caressed her stomach. She knew she would feel robbed if anything should happen to the baby—and so much more. She knew she had to take care of herself to protect this unborn child. She pushed herself upright as she heard Charles' footsteps on the stairs.

"Do you feel more rested now?" he asked as he entered the room.

"No. I'm exhausted. I might have been lying still, but I've been tossing and turning things over in my mind and trying to right the wrongs of the whole world. It's all very wearying."

"I'm sorry to hear that. Anything I can help with?"

"Oh, you know, the rights of women, the rights of the unborn child. Just small things really."

"Oh, nothing, then." He laughed. "Honestly, I can't leave you alone for a second, and you're worrying about everything. At least, Fred wasn't on that list."

"I suppose now that he's gone, there's nothing I can do about it."

"And you can about women's rights?"

"In a way, yes. I suppose I think that you have to keep on reminding people that the way it is now has got to change. Point out when you think somebody's doing wrong or, at least, try to help."

"Which is why we have our nephews practically living here."

"Well, I've long given up trying to change my father's mind, but I can at least help my mother. And Stuart and Henry are of the next generation. So, even if we can't change this one, maybe we can change the next."

Charles climbed into bed beside her. "Despite being forever worried about the strain you're putting on yourself, I cannot help but admire your fighting spirit. There's no preaching to the converted with you. You always have your mind on those who need changing."

"You see? Optimistic like Fred." She grinned. "The baby seems to agree with me, too. It's positively leaping. I don't think I'll get much sleep tonight. I'm sorry." She turned the lamp on her bedside table down and then off.

In the dark, Charles leaned across and said, "I hope this baby is a girl, and then you can guide her in whatever way you want. You can educate her and tell her that she can be whatever she wants to be."

"I'm so glad I married such an enlightened man," she said as she kissed him.

"Oh, so very enlightened. And now I think we should pray for a safe delivery and Fred's safety, too."

1907

IDAHO

The life they were now leading was so different from anything they had experienced before. When Fred and Niall had both arrived in the United States, of course, it was nothing like Ireland. Yet their jobs and the cities in which they lived were in some ways comparable— not to the actual places that they grew up in but not so completely dissimilar to a big city like Belfast. Fred simply worked in a shop, and Niall was still a carpenter.

It was true the buildings were bigger; but the bustle, the people, the buses and trams were the same. Philadelphia even boasted some history. And stuck on the edge of that great continent, if you had never experienced the vast tracts of land to the West, you might carry on your life without ever knowing there was so much more of America, that you were catching only such a small glimpse of the country which expanded so very far westward.

But Fred and Niall had decided to go, so they left the comparative safeness of the East Coast and ventured across the enormity of the continent, leaving Philadelphia in mid-September, ending up in Idaho almost at the end of that month. It had taken them as long to arrive there as it had for them to cross the Atlantic and almost the same distance, too—three thousand miles and all across the same country. There the similarities ended, though.

The journey by sea had, in some respects, been all the same, mile upon endless mile of waves and surf, changing color only ever so slightly, sometimes gray and occasionally blue. The journey across the States was endlessly different, though, the changes dramatic.

The first part, although long, was more familiar. They traveled back up to New York before going on to Chicago, up along the Hudson River, across by Lake Erie, and then over to the "Windy City" on Lake Michigan. The lakes were impressive. Fred could easily understand why they were called the Great Lakes. You could see the land a bit on the other side on Lake Erie but not with Lake Michigan. He knew that they were hundreds of miles in land but standing on the water's edge, it was like looking at the sea.

They stopped overnight in Chicago, as they had to change trains; and rather than always sleep in a train, they thought they might as well see what the other big cities of America were like. The wind whipped up around them as they stood on the shores of the lake and then turned to look at the city skyline rising up behind them, tall buildings dominating, the roads like wind tunnels down to the lake.

From there, they traveled again, through French-sounding places like Des Moines and places that had names that seemed like a contradiction in terms, like Council Bluffs—the one part sounding so officious, the other almost dangerous like a kind of cliff. Or perhaps it was a double bluff, a name to make you feel secure, a dampening down of the hazard, real though it might be. They stopped a night here, too. It was where the Transcontinental Railway began—or rather, met up with the railways that stretched back up to the East. They had even put in a golden spike to mark the spot where the two railroads met.

It had been open for only about thirty, maybe forty years and stood on the banks of the Missouri River. Almost the last thing the railroad had to do was to build a bridge to cross it. Even the river was bigger than anything Fred had ever seen as it wound its way down toward the South, meeting up with the Mississippi.

It was here that their journey really began—the Pacific Union Railway. They crossed the huge plains of Nebraska and entered into Wyoming, where the landscape began to change again—extraordinary, vast, rolling hills, as if a giant had once walked over the plains and, on entering Wyoming, let drop a thick, green, velvet cloak, which crumpled on the ground, mounds of material folding in and over itself. And then the hills became mountains—mile upon hundreds of miles as far as the eye could see and beyond of magnificent scenery.

Fred had never encountered anything like it before. And there was nobody in it. No houses, no farms—nothing except the railroad track and the mountains and the sky. Endless sky above and these were just the foothills of the Rockies, as they moved from Wyoming into Idaho with Washington beyond.

"Imagine coming here on a covered wagon," Niall said as they began to mount the Rockies, the train crawling up the ever-steeper slopes.

"Imagine building the railway," Fred replied.

"So true, but when they set off in their wagon trails, they must have really wanted something badly to go off like that to not worry that they might die."

"I think they must have had hope that life would be better. I mean, we crossed an ocean, and now we're still going West in the hope of a better life. It must have been the same for them. It's just all that land. There is just so much of it."

"I'm sure they did, but I don't think I'm so much of a pioneer that I would have come out here not knowing where I was going. Much better to go by train but still feel enterprising!"

Fred laughed. "I think I agree, but can you imagine those people carving their way through the mountains so we could get on a train at Council Bluffs and end up in Idaho? It beggars belief."

"We'll soon have to get used to explosions in those mines."

"Very different from telling a man he should buy a scarf." Fred grinned.

"Oh, so different. Mind you it's not much like carpentry either."

"You have to build props to stop the mine collapsing on top of you, though, don't you?"

"I think so, but that isn't the kind of carpentry I'm used to."

When Fred had first thought about mining in Philadelphia, he supposed he had considered it to be like coal mining. It was true; he had never been down a mine or, come to think of it, even met a miner; but he thought he knew what the experience was like. He didn't have any way of comparing his experience to that of a coal miner, but the silver mines, high up in the Rocky Mountains, were an experience in and of themselves.

The silver mine they headed to was in Mace. Niall's friends back in Philadelphia had told him about it. They had known someone who had gone and come back with tales of the riches that were to be made. Mace was a small settlement with just a few wooden houses in a dip between two hills. You couldn't really call it a valley; that implied something long and down low between the mountains, whereas this was a town—or so they called it—perched more on the side of a hill with a neighboring hill rising up on the other side. It was a small gap with just enough flat land to build on.

It had a boarding house, which the citizens called a hotel—and this was where they stayed—a saloon, a sheriff's office, a few more houses—most of them built down the one street—along with a general store and a church. The mine was built into the side of the mountain at the end of town. The entrance was carved into the bottom of the hill and looked innocuous from the outside, an unassuming door, albeit unusually placed; inside was a labyrinth of tunnels stretching far into the rock, along and down. Explosions shook the hillside; some so deep inside that nothing stirred above. Great wheels and cranks shifted and separated the debris from the precious metal.

Fred wasn't sure if he had made the right decision. After all, he had never done any kind of hard work like this before. But this was a land of possibilities, and Fred felt his anticipation growing as he saw a future with Niamh becoming closer to a reality.

It was very, very cold here. Snow covered the mountain tops and the forest; snow covered the rooftops, too—thick snow. It drifted up against the sides of the buildings so that if you stepped into it, you would disappear, engulfed by those dazzling, white flakes that had come down the night before. It reached up almost covering the walkways and between the buildings. Now, the sky was blue, a piercing, preternatural color that seemed to highlight all the sky above and the vast earth below.

Fred looked out of the window in the boarding house he was staying in with Niall. The scenery was magnificent. He tried to remember the word Niamh had called it. She was talking about a poet—Wordsworth! That was it—and she'd been saying how he'd felt as a small boy rowing across the water in the Lake District in England. She'd been looking at the landscape around the Giant's Causeway, and she used a word he hadn't heard in that context before. She'd explained that it meant that you felt both the beauty of the scenery but also a kind of fear, as if the thing before you could ravage you while remaining forever beautiful.

Sublime—that was it. The scene in front of him—those extraordinary craggy cliffs and the forests that went right up to them—was awe-inspiring. It was sublime. He knew the mountains could kill you. You could fall down a ravine, get lost in those swathes of forest. You could be attacked by a bear or suffocated in an avalanche. And yet, looking at them now, he was lost in a sense of wonder at their extraordinary majesty, terrifying or not. It was the sheer scale of them, peak after peak going on for what seemed an eternity.

That was it, really, he thought. It was like the Garden of Eden after the Fall with the presence of God presiding over it. Still beautiful but flawed, and humanity feeling infinitesimally small in His presence. Fred felt dwarfed into insignificance against the towering mountains of God's creation. He was overwhelmed. He had never felt so moved by scenery that both oppressed and yet uplifted at the same time. His own hopes and dreams faded into nothing beside the austere beauty of the Rockies. He felt he could look at them, always transfixed.

"Having deep thoughts again, are we?" asked Niall, who had awoken. He rubbed his eyes and stretched. "I can't say I blame you.

You feel you could put the whole of Ireland in just a part of it, and our mountains wouldn't even register as the foothills."

Fred turned away from the view at the window. "They are just so incredible. Well-named, too—the Rockies. They rise up all steep and rugged and jagged. They're just so enormous, they seem to fill the sky."

"Don't go poetic on me again. It's a good job. You've got the money to buy a ticket for Niamh. I don't think I could take any more of your looking out the window and getting philosophical, even though I do agree."

"It's just the sense of infinite space and us in comparison. If you didn't believe in the greatness of God, this would *have* to convince you."

"Fortunately for you—and, in fact, for me—I do believe in God, and it's the same One as you, despite our theological differences." He smiled. "But if we don't stop dwelling on the Almighty and start thinking about going to the mine one last time, all our theological thoughts won't get us anywhere."

"You are so right," said Fred, tearing himself away. "We had better get going. You don't fancy staying on now that I'm going? Get even richer?"

"No. Although I could earn a fortune," he joked. "I'm not convinced this is the life for me. Too much like hard work."

Whenever he entered the mine, Fred was reminded of that poem by Robert Browning Niamh had told him about, "The Pied Piper of Hamlin." In that poem, the piper had convinced the children of Hamlin to dance their way into a mountain, never to be seen again, as the entrance had closed behind them.

Fred's natural cheerfulness and optimism kept him from thinking that he, too, would be swallowed up, but even he had, on occasion, wondered whether or not that would be his fate. As the daylight disappeared from view and a small, flickering lamp was the only thing that helped him see where he was headed, armed with a pickaxe, it wasn't impossible to see why Niamh would be so concerned.

Niall was right, as well. It was too much like hard work. Hacking away into the rock hundreds of feet into the mountain was backbreaking. As different a way of earning a living as being a store assistant as could be imagined. The one so polite—so genteel almost—civil, and the other so bruising and physical. It had all been worth it, though. In just three short months, he had gained enough money to organize a transfer to his sister Hilda so that she could, in turn, give money to Niamh to buy a ticket to the States.

At first, he didn't know how he was going to do it. It seemed that he was now on the edge of the earth, Niamh safely at home in Ireland. The thought of transferring money had somehow felt easier in a city. There were banks where you could leave your money to save and, he had assumed, send the money back to Ireland.

To be honest, he hadn't actually thought about how he would do it, just assumed that the man in the bank would tell him. When he had been with Niamh and they had concocted their plan, they had just agreed he would send his earnings back to Hilda, who would give them to Niamh. It all seemed a little whimsical now.

When he had arrived in Philadelphia, though, he had opened a savings account; that was how he had managed to buy the ticket to Mace. But when he had arrived in Idaho, it had all become much more complicated. That was until a fellow miner had told him about

Western Union. Not a bank as such but they could still send money anywhere, it seemed, in the world, even to a small bank in Ireland with an account held by Charles Bell, his brother-in-law.

He could not help but be impressed. The business side of him was staggered at the efficiency of the whole process—that you could transfer money earned at the edge of nowhere and it could end up in Charles' bank. The whole world was connected through telegraphs. They even had one that went deep down across the very ocean that he had traveled on to get to America in the first place. It was just incredible. It shrank the world.

Shrank it in one sense, anyway. He still felt a million miles from Niamh, further than in Philadelphia. Yet it was to the West that he wanted her to come. He wanted to share with her this idyll, free from all the petty prejudices of home, away from the sectarian divides that would have meant they could never be together. He wished he had the power of language to express how he felt to her in his letters. He wanted some way of expressing how the nature around him made him feel. He supposed that that was how Wordsworth had landed on the word *sublime*, it was a word that conjured up both the landscape and his emotion. The trouble was that he wasn't a poet.

He remembered an incident that had happened to him when he first arrived. He'd gone out, early in the morning, walked some way off into the hills above the town. It was the very end of the summer, really, although, strictly speaking, it was autumn and he had sat down on a tree stump by a stream. He was completely, utterly alone. It was as if he was the first man who had ever encountered that stump, heard the brook, seen the dappling leaves ready to fall, when he glanced over and saw a deer stooping down, lapping up the clear water as it cascaded down the mountain.

The deer had looked up, straight over at him, without fear, stayed for a moment, and then went, leaping up the side of the hill. The incident was over before it had even begun. He had tried to describe it to Niamh, in a letter, but he could say only that he'd seen a deer up on the hill, which missed the point altogether—his feeling of his oneness with nature and its Maker. He supposed, on thinking about it, that it was a sense of peace—"the peace that passes all understanding" captured in that moment, alone on a hillside with a deer. But you couldn't really convey that in words. You had to be there and feel it, too.

That was why he wanted Niamh to live out here. He wanted to share with her the staggeringly beautiful landscape but also for her to understand that it brought with it the hope, almost the promise, of a fresh start—that she had traveled so far, precisely to leave the anxieties of Ireland thousands of miles away and turn toward a life in the future, problem-free, at peace.

"Now you've got the money, you're not going to live with Niamh, here are you?" Niall asked. "I mean, it's a mining town, with all that that implies."

They walked down the main street of Mace, over the small footbridge, and up toward the mine. On their last day, they weren't going to go down the mineshaft, just sort out some equipment that had got jammed and needed unjamming—something electric that meant that the trundles had stopped going and were blocking the way deep down inside the mine.

"I was thinking of Spokane at first. It's more of a proper town than Mace, fewer rampaging miners of a night. But ultimately, maybe she'd like to live by the sea again, go to Seattle or Vancouver."

"I can see you've got it all planned."

"I have indeed. When I've finished work, I'm taking myself off to a hotel in Spokane to look for a place to live. You're more than welcome to join me; you know that, don't you? Niamh won't get here for at least a month, if not more, and so you won't be intruding. Besides, we've got to have a witness when we get married. You've got to come back with me to New York for that."

"And I promise you I'll be there for that, but for now, I want to do a bit of exploring. I think I'll go to San Francisco and have a look around before coming back up, if that's all right with you."

"That's absolutely fine. I think Niamh will be very relieved to see that the only real friend I've made in the States is a Catholic, just like her!" Fred punched Niall on the arm. "So, now, tell me how on earth do we sort out this problem? I know it's easier than chipping away at rock, but I have to say I'm a bit apprehensive today. I don't know why. I have to sort out something to do with the electric power being intermittent on the lift shaft."

1908

Ireland

Niamh had gone straight away after school to buy the ticket that would take her to America. She had told no one there, not even Erin. The check that Charles had written sat all day in her bag. Every time she looked at it, the leather seemed to become see-through as if everyone in class or in the staff room knew what was in there, a piece of paper advertising her intention to leave the country.

She had found out where to get her ticket, the price, and what agency to go to as soon Hilda had told her that the money had come into Charles' bank account. It was here. Fred had transferred enough money for her to travel to the States. Under a year after he had left, she would be following in his footsteps, going across to Liverpool and then over to New York. It was almost impossible, too incredible to believe that she was going, but it was true. Hilda had just hugged her for so long.

"I can't believe that you'll see him again. I have so much for you to take to see him, including the photograph of wee Mary. I've told him that she was born, but I want him to see a picture of her. It will be out of date by the time you get there, but I want him to see a picture of her, anyway. She has his green eyes—not that you can see that in the picture but tell him about her."

She hugged Niamh again, almost delirious with excitement. It was as if she were hugging Fred by proxy, a brother she would never see again, so Niamh would have to be him for a moment. When she broke away from her, Niamh saw there were tears in her eyes.

"I know it's stupid, but when Fred left I couldn't help but just feel sad—sad that he was leaving, sad that my parents more or less threw him out, sad for you. Just sad. And now, I can feel happy again. It's all worked out. I mean, of course I'm sorry that you're leaving, but these tears are happy ones. Honestly. I'm so glad that you're going."

"I know," Niamh replied, her eyes welling up, too. "But now, of course, I'm going to have to tell my parents, and I don't know how they will react. Certainly not like you. Not only am I going to say that I'm leaving, which is bad enough, but I'm also going to have to say that I never broke the engagement."

She had decided that buying the ticket first was the best way to do it. She wouldn't have to stop and think about what she was leaving behind—her home, her family, her work. She would think about all that after she had purchased it. She knew the most difficult thing to do was to tell her parents, let them know that in all those months of anxiety they had experienced about her broken heart, she had still been in touch with him, hadn't ever broken the engagement, and was now going to join him.

If she had bought the ticket, she thought, the fact of her going would seem more like a *fait accomplis*, not something that could be negotiated. So, the buying of it had not been that difficult. She had just blocked everything out of her mind except the fact that in just over a month, she would be with Fred.

He was going to meet her in New York, where they would be married, and then they would travel west together and start a new life—at first in Spokane, moving only if she wanted, to the coast, even Canada. Fred had asked his friend Niall to be a witness at their wedding, and Niall had persuaded him to get married in a Catholic church.

This, to Niamh, was a huge concession. Without it, she felt as if she wouldn't really have a husband in the eyes of God. It was strange, but she thought a ceremony without mass, without a priest, wasn't really a marriage at all. She knew that Fred was still resolutely Protestant and couldn't imagine what it must take for him to concede. He had tried to tell her in his last letter.

> *I know that getting married in a Catholic church is more important to you than it is to me. There are so many denominations amongst the Protestants that I will just have to consider that we are all part of one catholic church. I think that's what the Anglicans say in communion. I just won't think that the bread and wine are actually Christ's body and blood, like you. But the Almighty God will understand that we want to get married in His sight, and that's what's important.*

She felt, though, making that decision must have been easier in America than it was in Ireland. In Ireland, she knew, he would have had to convert to Catholicism, there being no way they could exist one Protestant, one Catholic living as man and wife. Without the deep divisions, the sectarian war that lived barely beneath the surface of everyday life, it might be easier.

Explaining to her parents that she was going to have a Catholic wedding would also be good, as long as she didn't have to go on to admit Fred still thought everything about Catholicism was wrong and was doing it only because he loved their daughter and because he believed, in his words, that an Almighty God would understand.

What Fred couldn't see was that taking the Eucharist together, believing that the bread and wine were Christ's body and blood, unified them and brought them together in His actual lived presence. She wondered if, when the marriage was taking place, whether or not she would notice, or if the sheer pleasure at being reunited with him would banish any fears that she might now have.

As she began to contemplate what she might be thinking of during the wedding, she began to feel nervous. At first, she thought it was a sense of fear, linked to her worries about telling her parents. But then, as the apprehension grew, she realized that while, in part. it was of course that, it was also the kind of fear that was linked to anticipation as well. As she sat on the bus and then the train, the ticket now almost burning a hole in her bag, it was as if her whole body was acknowledging the emotion going on inside her before she had even had a chance to consider what it was.

As the train approached Toombe Bridge, Niamh was gripped by a feeling that she had not had since she first started walking out with Fred. It could be described only as butterflies. She remembered the second time she had seen him, waiting for him at Hilda's house, unsure if he would find an excuse to call at the end of the women's suffrage meeting. She had felt that same nervous apprehension she was now feeling, though now she had to admit it was worse.

They called it butterflies, she assumed, because you felt a kind of light fluttering feeling so faint that only butterfly wings, not birdwings, could produce it. The sensation she felt, though, was more like a bird trapped in a room with no way to get out, flying one way and then the other, confused and almost panicking. She prayed that she would feel released when she had told her parents—like the bird finally escaping through a window—but she knew that the physical awareness of her eagerness in seeing Fred would not go away, that her desire marked out by that fluttering, even of a butterfly's wings, would persist.

Her mother, Aoife, was setting the table as Niamh walked in; her father had a volume of Yeats poetry open in front of him.

"Just listen to what this poet has said at the start of his new book. He said, 'I convinced myself that I should never go for the scenery of a poem to any country but my own, and I think that I shall hold to that conviction to the end.' Now, that's a fine statement if ever I heard one. And he was a Protestant, too."

It was as if, on entering, she had been given the perfect opening to her announcement, or at least an opening that would allow for her parents to think that some good could be found in the Protestant community. But in starting to tell them, she was still all too hesitant, stumbling over what she had to say.

"About that."

"About what?" her mother and father chimed together.

"About a Protestant making such a fine statement."

"What about it?"

In turning the words around, Niamh once again began to doubt her ability to say anything. She was silent too long.

"What are you trying to tell us?" her father asked. His voice, while not accusatory, still had the tone of a schoolmaster wanting to get to the bottom of a problem. "This is not about the poetry of Yeats, is it?"

She looked over at him. He was no longer relaxed in his chair but was sitting upright, turning toward her. Her mother had placed the cutlery down on the table in a bunch, not separated out in their places. She wondered if they had already guessed what was coming next, if they had shared secret conversations about her over the last year.

"So, come on now; what is this about? Why is it good that Yeats is proud of Ireland, even though he's Protestant?"

She knew then that he was leading her into confessing, as he would a pupil who had stolen an apple or been fighting with another child. She froze in his glare.

"It's about that boy, isn't it? This is about Fred. What has he done?"

Niamh didn't say anything. The ticket was there, in the bag that she now was clutching. All she had to do was tell them, fill in the gaps that they had clearly suspected. But she couldn't.

Part of the reason that her father, Aiden, made such a good headmaster was that for all his discipline, he cared about his charges, cared even more about his daughter, and was proud of all she had achieved. Behind the glare was a genuine desire to understand why the person had done wrong and try and put it right. The difficulty that Niamh had was that he thought the wrong had been righted when Fred had been sent away.

Father changed his approach. "Come on. You can tell us. He's halfway around the world and been gone nearly a year. It can't be that bad."

Niamh suddenly realized that they must have thought that she had heard something about him, that, perhaps, he had found someone else. Not that the someone else was her.

She stumbled again, looked down at her feet and then blurted it out, all at once. "It is about him, yes. I've bought a ticket to go to New York and marry him. But it's in a Catholic church, and his best friend there is Irish and Catholic, too. And we're going from New York to Spokane, which is on the West Coast—well, near it, anyway—and we're going to live there." She looked up again, breathless.

Her parents were both looking at her, incredulous.

"It's too late for me to back down now. The ticket was really expensive, and I'm not handing it back. Besides, I really don't think you can."

"You must have been planning this for a long time," her mother said quietly. "How did you do that?"

"I have, but the how isn't important. What's more important is that I am going, and I would rather go with your blessing than without it," she said, finally getting to the point.

Her father remained silent for a long time, and then he spoke, not sternly but with a gravity that was almost worse and with a look of hope dashed by disappointment.

"When I gave you an education, I did it because I wanted you to be able to survive without having to be dependent on men to look after you. And I think I've done that. You are an independent woman with views and ideas of your own and a woman who is campaigning for even more rights for women in the future.

"If you have decided to go and be with this Fred, there is nothing I can do to stop you; and I'm glad you have told us now and not just sneaked off in the night and told us when you had arrived. But if you are asking me if I agree with what you have done, then that will never happen.

"Yeats might be arguing for Home Rule, but he is, and always will be, a Protestant. Fred may let you get married in a Catholic church, but he isn't even in Ireland, let alone a Catholic. The Brethren are about as Protestant as you can get. They're the opposite to us, yet you still want to marry him. I just cannot approve."

Niamh tried not to cry, but as he spoke, she could feel, despite herself, tears rolling down her cheeks. She felt that she had failed the man she most admired, other than Fred.

"I am sorry," she said. "But I have to go."

"I know," Father said quietly. "And that is why I am going to give you my blessing, even though I think that what you are doing is absolutely wrong—and I mean that!" A hint of sternness had returned to his voice

Niamh began to sob. "Thank you. Thank you so much."

"I couldn't have it on my conscience that I had sent my daughter across the sea without my blessing. I only hope that God will understand. I'll be doing Hail Marys now until I die. Maybe I shouldn't have given you so much education after all." A hint of a smile crossed his face as Mother went across and drew Niamh toward her.

"I might not be there for the wedding," she said, squeezing Niamh's hand. "But I'm going to buy a dress for you to wear, and then I won't just imagine you in it. I'll know what it's like. And who knows? If he's willing to be married in a Catholic church, maybe, just maybe . . . "

Niamh didn't say anything more, and they didn't speak of it again over dinner. There was time to tell her younger brother Michael and two sisters, Josephine and Braid. The girls were busy regaling everyone at the table of an incident at school, and Michael was telling them of a letter he had received from their brother Connor, who was away at University in Dublin and had written to him that he should go there next year. It was as if the conversation was taking place in another room in the house. Niamh felt herself distant from it, drifting in and out, even when Michael asked her opinion.

"So, do you think I should go, Niamh? Niamh, do you think I should go? Niamh, is your head in the clouds?"

"Sorry. Yes, of course I think you should go." And then she drifted off again, her mind full of hope blotted with anxiety.

Only when dinner was past and Niamh was alone in the kitchen did her mother come in and say, "It's through his sister, isn't it? The one who runs that suffragist group."

Niamh nodded.

"And is that the reason that you go? Just so you can get letters from him?"

"No, it really isn't. I believe in what I'm doing there. But she has helped, and Fred sent the money to her husband's bank. That's how I bought the ticket."

"And you had this planned from the very beginning?"

"I'm so sorry I didn't tell you, but you were so angry when I told you we were engaged. I thought you would agree in the end; but you didn't, and I do so love him. I couldn't think of a life without him."

"Oh, Niamh, you've been lying to us for the best part of a year."

"Not exactly lying. Just not letting you know what I was really feeling. There were numerous times when I almost told you, but in the end, I didn't dare."

"I don't know if I feel angry at the deception or sorry that you couldn't tell us what you felt; disappointed that you would reject your faith or grateful that this man, whom you love so much, still loves you and has given you the money to go all the way to America to marry him."

Niamh looked down and started to cry again. Her mother came over to her and stroked her cheek.

"It must have been very difficult for you. I know. And I am going to buy that wedding dress for you. I am because I want some part of this huge decision that you're taking without ever once telling me you were going to do it."

"I am sorry—so very, very sorry—but if I had, you'd have said no, as you did the first time."

Mother nodded. "We almost certainly would have. I suppose you could see the fact that you're going to America is almost a punishment to us. We probably will never see you again, yet if you'd stayed here, you couldn't have married. The tensions between our communities are too great, never mind anything else. How will you manage without that community, without us? It's so different for a man, but a girl needs her mother."

"I'll miss you more than I can say. I will; of course, I will." Niamh was now crying. "But I want to be with Fred more than anything else, and we will work it out somehow. You'll see."

Her mother piled up the last of the dishes and put them up on the dresser. She appeared deep in thought.

"Your father has given his blessing, even though he doesn't approve, and you are my treasured oldest daughter, whom I love dearly. I will miss you more than life itself, but if you tell me that you are going to make it work, even though I have no idea how, then I will have to trust that you can. As your father says, you are an independent woman capable of anything. Like him, I can never agree with your decision, but I won't say anything more about it. So, tomorrow, we will go and buy you that dress, in which I am sure you will look beautiful, and you can send home a picture of you wearing it with Fred by your side."

Niamh went over and hugged her mother, sobbing into her shoulder. "Thank you," she mumbled. "Thank you so much."

16

"I KNEW THEY WOULDN'T TAKE it well," Hilda said.

"There's not taking it well, and there's *really* not taking it well, though. And they *really* didn't take it well. I suppose you can see why your father is still angry at Fred, and now, he won't speak to you or me either."

Hilda and Charles had finally sat down in the living room; the baby had just gone to sleep, coddled safely in sheets under blankets in the crib. Her small head was cradled in a cap Hilda's mother had made for her, her eyes fastly shut.

Hilda looked at the photograph of Fred with his two brothers. That was where the whole thing had begun, the romance between Fred and Niamh. Niamh had been attracted to him before she had even met him, described his expression as wistful.

Hilda looked at it again. She supposed she could see why Niamh thought that. It was really that he was in two minds about having it taken at all, and she supposed that at the moment the shutter came down, the photographer had caught the ambiguity he felt about his father wanting only the sons to be preserved in print, not the daughters—and, in particular, not Martha, a sister whom he would never see again. Whenever she looked at the photograph, she could see only Fred's sadness mixed in with his determination ever to look on the bright side.

She turned to Charles. "I think it was the fact he knew we'd helped."

"Yes, but you've only just had a baby and need your mother, and all he could do was to shout at you, waving that enormous family Bible and quoting the Ten Commandments. He kept berating you and asking how you had honored your father and your mother in what you'd done."

"He was awful to you as well, though."

"Yes, but they are not my parents, just in law. I can't say I enjoyed being told that I was a dreadful influence on you, but at least, he's not my father. He is yours, though. And what's worse is that he's going to bring the whole thing up among the elders with a view to asking us to leave the Assembly."

"I know." Hilda took in a deep breath. "And the difficulty with that is that the only way to avoid being cast out is to say we're sorry. You know, repent of our sins. And I'm not sorry. I'm not sorry at all. I know Niamh is a Catholic, but she's almost too good for Fred. She's educated, has a degree, and is a teacher. Fred left school at fourteen, and Niamh liked him, nonetheless. Of course, I was going to help him court her. I liked them both too much to say no."

Charles reached out and hugged her. "The problem is that you think of her as a woman and not a Catholic woman, and your father can see only the latter and none of the former about her. He can never know her for who she really is, only her faith, her beliefs. I know you don't think your father is very political . . . "

"He isn't," she interrupted him. "I know it's impossible in some ways not to be, but he isn't an Orangeman. He thinks it's wrong to turn the Gospel into something political."

"I know. That's true. So, he's not an Orangeman, but when he's asked about what should happen to Ireland, he's definitely not in favor of Home Rule, is he? For him, that's a Catholic idea, and he must feel threatened by the thought that the Catholics want Ireland to be independent, which would leave him living in a Catholic country, where there would be very little space for the Brethren. And Niamh is a Catholic. He can see his whole life slipping away from him, and now your brother, in his eyes, wants to join them."

"But she's a person as well. And you can't have her representing the whole of Catholic Ireland. That's just ridiculous, and Fred doesn't want to become a Catholic either. He may have gone for a bit more structure in the Presbyterians, but a Catholic? Never." Hilda raised her voice and then, all at once, listened to see if Mary had been roused from her sleep.

"It's a very good job that they don't know he's getting married in a Catholic church and that his new best friend is a man called Niall," Charles whispered as he waited to see if they could hear Mary stir.

"Don't. At least he knows something of our parents that he didn't tell them that. It was bad enough that we called our baby Mary. My father had images of all those pious-looking statues with a bright red heart. My mother had to persuade him that she was named that because I wanted to call her Martha, like my sister who died, and then just couldn't." She looked down for the briefest of moments, her voice catching. "I would call her after her sister Mary. And," she added more firmly, "Mary was the better sister, anyway."

"I wish I could believe that you think that on theological grounds, not that she wouldn't help her sister with the catering! But really, what are you going to say when the elders ask you if you are sorry you helped your brother against your father's wishes?"

"I suppose"—she sighed—"that I will just have to be honest."

"And say . . ."

"It's a shame that my mother is so browbeaten and cowed that she barely spoke a word. I know that she wants to be reconciled to Fred, no matter what he's done, and the thought that I won't be able to take Stuart and Henry off her hands will exhaust her. But of course, my father doesn't care about that. He won't volunteer to step up and help her. He's too busy doing what he thinks the Good Book says without seeing it from her point of view.

"He's not exactly loving her as Christ loved the Church, running her into the ground like he does. He reckons that wives should obey their husbands and children their parents, and that's that. He misses the fact that husbands are meant to love their wives as their own bodies and that parents aren't meant to provoke their children to anger. I hardly think that sending Fred away to America and now refusing to speak to me isn't provoking either of us to anger!"

Charles took her by the hands. "I couldn't agree with you more, and I love you for being this way, but you still haven't said what you will say to the elders. I'm not sure they would appreciate your preaching to them on the apostle Paul, even if in doing so, you are being honest and a better theologian than your father—and probably them as well."

"Are you telling me that I am going to have to say I'm sorry," she cried, outraged.

"Of course not. No. But we are going to have to work out a way of appearing regretful, while at the same time supporting Fred, and that will take some doing."

Hilda got up from the chair with a look of fatigue.

"I am too tired and cross to think about it now. I'm going to be awake again in a couple of hours and probably once more after that.

I think he's counting on my being too exhausted to argue. You can stay up and ponder upon it; and who knows, maybe inspiration will strike me at two o'clock this morning. But for now, I am going to go to sleep."

She went upstairs to get ready for bed, and she looked down at Mary in her crib. The blankets covering her rose and fell with every breath she took. On occasion, there was a pause before the next breath was taken, so profound was her sleep; and yet in two hours, she would awake, crying for her next feed. Hilda cupped her tiny face in her hands.

"Don't worry. I won't provoke you to anger when you grow up. I will always be there, no matter what you do; and even if I think it's wrong, I will never send you away to America, and I will never say you have to leave the Assembly."

Mary, as if responding to her mother, breathed deeply.

"Bless you, sweet thing. Bless you."

Hilda sipped her tea, which still steamed. Charles had already left for work, and Mary was contentedly staring up at the ceiling, making an odd gurgling sound, when someone knocked at the door. Hilda rose and went over to open it, surprised that anyone was coming to see her quite so early in the morning.

As she drew back the latch, she saw her mother standing there with a look of determination about her that was remarkable. She had never seen her mother look so firm, almost in charge. She was used to her appearing exhausted and weary, pale and anemic. But now, beneath the hat she was wearing was a look of resolution as if, at last, she was going to have her say.

"Well, aren't you going to ask me in? It's very cold out here."

"Yes, yes, of course, I am. I thought you weren't allowed to see me, though, 'til after the meeting."

Her mother, Edith, entered, taking off her coat as she came. "I'm not, but I've decided to take a leaf out of your book and let the women have a say in the decision. I've lost a daughter to appendicitis and a son to America, and I'm not going to lose another daughter as well. I've got Jane speaking to Matthew and Emily talking to Harold, and we're going to fight it."

"And have you spoken to Father?"

"No, not yet; but when I do, I will tell him that I knew Fred was writing to Niamh."

"But you didn't." Hilda gasped, astonished.

"Do you think that those two small boys said nothing to me all these months?"

"They didn't know, though. We were so careful. We always waited until they were out in the garden if Niamh was coming around; and when we had the women's meetings, there were others there, too, so they can't have known."

"If you think you can hide all your secrets from two highly inquisitive, not to say nosy boys, then you have another thing coming," said Mother with conviction. "Of course, I didn't know absolutely what was planned or how regularly she was getting letters, but I knew from the moment Fred gave in so easily that there was something happening. Nobody plucks up that amount of courage to tell your father that he's going to marry a Catholic and then says just a few days later that it's fine and that he'll be glad to go to America.

"I think I actually knew something was going on before he even told us he was engaged. Stuart had seen Fred with a girl about six months before he said anything. At first, I just thought that he was walking out with a girl, and it wasn't that serious; but the minute he said that Niamh was a Catholic, I realized that was who Stuart had seen him with."

Hilda sat there, incredulous. "Why didn't you say anything?"

"Because I didn't think that your father would take it out on you as well as Fred. Up until now, I've been writing to Fred because in your father's eyes, he'd repented; but now, he knows he hasn't. And what's more, you've helped Fred. Your father is beside himself. He is so angry, but I am not going to lose you, too."

She paused. "I want you to know that I don't agree with what Fred has done, and I am not wholly sympathetic with you either; but I have to confess that I didn't say anything when I could have, and that's what I am going to tell your father. If he has to cast you out, he has to cast me out as well; and however irate he is now, he won't do that, particularly as Jane and Emily are speaking to Matthew and Harold."

"Women unite!" said Hilda, crying. "You cannot imagine how grateful I am to you. I will be forever in your debt and look after Stuart and Henry permanently if you wish, although I will watch them much more carefully now. I am so, so grateful."

"As I say, don't suppose that I agree with you. Niamh is a Catholic, and you would have been better telling him that it won't work in the end, rather than helping him to write letters and save up to marry her. Though, you might have something with the women thing. Standing together is a whole lot easier than trying to do everything on your own when you're too tired to even think. Speaking of, how much sleep are you getting at night?"

"Don't worry about me. I'm young, and Mary is doing fine. She wakes up only twice in the night, and she settles back down easily once she's fed."

"I don't want you getting as worn out as I was, though."

"The difference is that I don't have eleven children, and I have a loving husband who helps and looks after me—not a husband who thinks my only job is childbearing with a whole lot of cooking and cleaning thrown in for good measure."

"You shouldn't be so harsh on him. He is faithful and hard-working, admittedly not in the home but very hardworking at his job. And he provides sufficiently for all of us to live. It can't be easy making enough money to feed such a large household; and we have always managed, and that is down to him. He is a real believer in the parable of the talents. He has worked hard with the talents God has given him. I think Fred has a bit of that in him as well. It can't have been straightforward, getting all that money together in such a short space of time. There must be something of the canny businessman in him, too."

"All I can say is that my father is lucky to have married you. It's hard to be gracious to a man who wants to cast you out from his church when you're his eldest daughter."

"I understand. I do. But you have to realize that he thinks he's doing God's will, not his own. He kept talking about Abraham and Isaac last night. I think he thinks he's Abraham."

"Well, as long as you and Jane and Emily persuade the men in your life that he's not, I can forgive him."

Mother rose and kissed Hilda on the top of her head. "And I hope that, in time, he can forgive you, too." She walked down the hall to the door, putting on her coat, and, as she opened it, she was confronted by a man holding a telegraph addressed to Mrs. Bell.

"I have a telegraph for you, madam," he said.

"I think it's meant for my daughter," she replied. "Hilda."

Hilda crossed to the hall, saying, "Thank you" to the gentleman as she took the telegram extended to her.

She stared at the envelope. A strange disquiet came over her as she said goodbye to the messenger. It could be from only Fred, but he had already sent the money and a letter. Niamh was packed and waiting to sail to Liverpool.

She looked across at her mother, who took off her coat again and went inside, back into the kitchen. Wee Mary cooed and then smiled as her grandmother placed her on her knee.

"You have to open it," she urged Hilda.

"I don't think I can. It can't be good news. No one ever sends a telegram with good news in it."

"It might be Fred just wanting to know how your father has taken the news."

"He wouldn't send a telegram for that, though, would he? I can't bear it. And why would he send it to me and not Niamh? He could send it to her home now that he knows she's coming. I have this awful feeling."

She placed the envelope on the table. Unopened, it threatened to tell her something dreadful had happened. It wasn't conclusive. She could still imagine that it contained other news. Opened, it would reveal the truth, the stark reality that a fatal accident had occurred.

Hilda glanced down at her mother and Mary, sitting so prettily in her mother's arms. She was looking up, beaming, her fat cheeks dimpled with the smile.

"If you want, I can open it," her mother said.

"It's all right. I can do it." Trembling, she lifted the telegram out of the envelope. At first, she couldn't take it in, and then she read again the full horror of it, spelled out in so few words. Hilda dropped the telegram and crumpled to the floor, letting out a howl. Mother carefully lay Mary down and, weeping, clutched Hilda, rocking and hugging her as she swayed back and forth, wailing.

17

"I CAN'T SEE WHY YOU have to go to America. Stay here with us," her mother begged.

But Niamh was clear. "I have to see where he was. I have to go and see how he lived out his last year, and I have to go to the place where he died. I do."

"But he's not there anymore. He's gone, and it will only prolong your grief if you go. We'll look after you. You'll be with the people who know and love you, not strangers who have never met you. How will you be able to grieve with people you don't know?"

"Because I have to be able to see and feel what he saw and believed in, even if it didn't come true. And I have the ticket."

She was resolute in her misery, and in the end, her parents finally acquiesced; but they were firm in one thing.

"Even though we can't prevent you from leaving, we want you to come home," Father said. "So, we have bought you a return ticket."

As Niamh started to protest, he held up his hand.

"On this point, there is to be no discussion. We have just enough for a third-class ticket, and we have bought it. We will allow you to stay for up to two months, and then you are coming back. Fred's parents may have been glad to see the back of their son, but we don't want to say goodbye to our daughter. So, you are coming home. Do you understand?" His voice started to crack as he spoke.

"I still don't see why you are going," he continued, "but you are, and we will support you in all you do. I will accompany you to Liverpool, and my second cousin Padraig and his wife, Sinead, who are going to emigrate to America, are going to be with you on the journey over."

Again, Niamh started to resist, but Father was firm. "I'm not going to have my grieving daughter go all the way to the States on her own, and that's final. I'd take you myself, only I can't just up and leave the school. And I can't really afford it. So, that's that."

There was one other person that she felt she had to tell and explain why she was leaving her job to go to the United States—Erin, her oldest friend—the friend she used to tell everything to and then stopped. It was too awkward, difficult, and even painful to admit that she had fallen for a Protestant. And the longer the relationship had lasted, the more impossible it was to tell her until, of course, she had to when she resigned.

Niamh could have told her that Fred had been killed without telling her he was a Protestant, but she knew that Erin would ask why she hadn't told her about him all these months, why she had been so secretive about it all. Erin knew her too well and would realize the tension that had been mounting between them had been centered around a man—Fred. She would have known, without Niamh having to say anything at all. So, Niamh told her.

Erin's anger was incandescent. Niamh called at her house straight after she had submitted her letter to Sister Bernadette. "Niamh, what a pleasant surprise. Do come in for a cup of tea."

"No, thank you." Niamh looked down at her hands. "I want to tell you something, and I think we should go for a walk," she stumbled, her voice cracking.

"Let me get my hat and coat." When Erin returned to Niamh, she saw that her friend had become pale, all the color drained from her face. Niamh started to tremble.

"Oh, my goodness, whatever is the matter?" she asked as she closed the door behind her. "Has someone died?"

Niamh began to sob, one gulp of air followed by another, gasping for breath until she could cry no more.

Erin took her in her arms and hugged her tightly. "Oh, you poor dear, cry as much as you want." Still holding Niamh, she asked, "Who has died? Is it your mother, your father, one of your brothers or sisters? Who is it? You poor thing."

And then Niamh told her.

Erin pushed her away and stood there, looking at her.

"A Protestant!" she screamed. "You fell in love with a Proddy? A Proddy! How could you? How could you? A Proddy! All that stuff about votes for women, and really, it was just because of a man. Sneaking around behind everyone's back. You and your precious group of women—all Protestants. And here we are, fighting for Home Rule." Her face flared as red as her hair, spittle in her mouth. "I can hardly bear to look at you. Traitor. Get away from me; or I'll have the boys on you, and you'll be tarred and feathered."

She paused, suddenly, taking a breath. Without looking at Niamh, she said, coldly, "Go, or I might do or say something I regret. Go. Now." And she stormed back into the house, slamming the door behind her so hard, it barely stayed on its hinges.

Niamh slumped against the wall of Erin's home, her hands on her knees, staring blankly, breathing deeply. She knew Erin wouldn't tell her Fenian friends about what she had done—at least she hoped she wouldn't—but it seemed this was the end of any friendship she would ever have with her. The breach she had caused was too deep ever to be rectified. She dredged herself upright and walked home in a daze.

Niamh gazed down at the quayside and then out at the city beyond. It was gray. Everything she could see was gray. The sky, the sea, the quay, the buildings—even the sound around her seemed gray and dreary, dismal. The funnel had belched smoke as they drew into the harbor, and the foghorn had let out a doleful toll. It was funereal. It held no promise.

People far below scurried back and forth along the quay with trollies, pushing and shoving their way through the crowds that had gathered as the ship finally docked and the gantries began to descend. So, this was New York, the bright and brilliant city, shining with an expectation that was now thwarted. She turned and looked at the people who were beginning to disembark. The wealthiest went first, wrapped up in furs and muffs, ushered off to waiting individuals who piled up their trunks and pushed them away through the throng. Next was the second class, carrying their large cases, searching for people they knew down below. Niamh began to walk toward the gantry that would take her onto American soil.

Suddenly, she stopped. It was all too much, too awful. This was meant to be a joyful experience, meeting Fred as she got off the ship, embracing him and then heading off to a church to get married, with Niall as the best man. But now this. Alone, so very alone, determined to see the place that had given Fred such hope for it all to be taken away.

She choked as the people behind pushed forward. She was not going to cry, even though she could feel the tears welling up inside her. She gulped down a sob as she felt her shoulders heave. She was not going to cry. She was not going to cry. Niamh shook her head, inhaled deeply, and began the long walk down to the quayside.

At least, she was meeting Niall—not that she really knew what he looked like, but he would be able to recognize her. She was to wear a circular hat with feathers and pale pink roses gathered around the front rim. She had chosen it as a surprise for Fred. She'd tried one on that was very similar but had not bought it.

"It frames your face, and the pink brings out the color in your cheeks!" he'd said as he'd stroked them.

Oh, Fred. She could feel herself starting to cry again as she clasped the hat. So, she held herself upright and carried on down the gangway, knowing it would be she who would recognize Niall, rather than the other way around, because he was going to hold up a sign with his name on it, large and bold, that said "Niall Sweeney." There were too many people for her to see anybody—porters shouting for custom men, women jostling, small children running in and out between the crowds. It was overwhelming as she slowly made her way through to the front. She wondered if they would ever find each other.

It had seemed simpler in Toombe, even though her parents had been against her going.

Padraig and Sinead had been kind on the weeklong journey to New York. They didn't intrude but were always there if she needed to be distracted, to talk about nothing in particular. They had been told some of the circumstances under which Niamh was traveling but not all—not the most significant as far as her father and mother were concerned—that she had been going to marry a Protestant. They had just shared that Niamh was to marry; and now, her fiancé had died tragically, and she was going to see where he was buried before coming home again. The fact that she was to be met by a man named Niall helped in the illusion that Fred had been Catholic.

But now, Padraig and Sinead had to wait on the ship for the ferry to Ellis Island, so Niamh had to disembark on her own. She suddenly thought that this was what Fred must have done as well, stayed on the ship until he could go through to Ellis Island, ferried away with all the other hordes waiting to gain entry to the Promised Land.

She entered the main concourse of the terminal, praying that Niall had received her letter and would be there.

Suddenly, she heard a cry. "Niamh! Niamh, is that you?"

She craned to see who the caller was. She saw a man waving a huge notice in front of him that said, "Niall Sweeney." Fred had never described him to her but had spoken a great deal of him. He was tall with dark, wavy hair, very blue eyes, and pale skin. He wasn't particularly good-looking, his chin disappearing into his neck; but when he smiled, he seemed honest and trustworthy—and she would have to trust him, as he was to be her guide over the next two months.

"Let me take your bags for you, will you?"

"Thank you. Thank you very much," she replied. "I'm Niamh."

"Of course, you are. I've a room for you in a hotel in Manhattan, which will be grand. And tomorrow, I'll show you the sights before we get the train tomorrow night."

She nodded in assent, unable to speak.

"He was a terrific man, your Fred. Ever the optimist," Niall added hastily. "We can talk about him if you want—or not. It's up to you."

She hesitated. "Maybe later. I think I just want to go and find my room and be on my own. It's very good of you to come and meet me—and even more, to take me to his grave. I know it's a long way that you had to come back."

"It's nothing. I had a return ticket, anyway, so it was no problem; and money was no difficulty. We made a fair bit in those mines." He paused. "You'll go back a richer woman than you came. I've got all the money Fred was going to put on building a house out in Spokane."

Niamh looked up at him and smiled. "Fred always said you were a good man. I'm sure that many would have said the money all went on the fares and pocketed the rest. I'm so glad he met you. At least, I know he had a good friend when he was here."

Niall nodded. "And I had a very good friend in him. Of course, I wasn't going to take his money. It's all for you. It's all for you. Now, come on. I've got to get you to the Hotel Astor. You're going to be put up in style."

When she saw the hotel, Niamh knew that this must be where they had been going to stay for the wedding night. It was far too grand for just a place to stay before catching a train. The hotel was big enough already, yet they were adding to it. Soon, it would occupy a whole block. New York was an enormous grid—avenues going one way, streets at a perpendicular, each going off to the horizon yet all hemmed in by vast buildings, so big they almost blocked out the light.

She lay on the bed. It was so different. The sense of loss was more acute than ever it had been in Ireland. Perhaps her mother had been right after all. The emptiness was complete. Fred was not here and never would be, and it seemed all the more intense in a city where he should have been, where they should now be celebrating their wedding. The words of the telegram came back to her.

FRED DEAD STOP ELECTROCUTED AT MINE STOP HEARTFELT SORROW STOP NIALL

It hadn't even been sent to her. She knew why, of course, but the abruptness of the language and the mechanical nature of the wording had broken her heart when Hilda had called around to show it to her. Niall had attempted to soften the blow in the last two words, but she had been able to take in only the first two. Fred was dead.

All her fears about his being crushed in a mining accident had failed to materialize, but still, it had been the mine that had killed him. Her father had consoled her with the fact that it must have been quick, so quick he wouldn't have known anything about it; but that didn't matter at all because it was an accident in the mine that had ended his life at the age of twenty-three. She stared bleakly at the ceiling until slowly, she drifted off into a troubled sleep.

SHE SAW THE SIGHTS OF New York the following day, in a kind of daze. They walked, it seemed, miles up Fifth Avenue, although it was only fifteen blocks. They didn't speak much. Niamh took it all in a mesmeric trance, Niall occasionally pointing out something along the way until they arrived in a square in front of the park that had another huge hotel on one side of it, the Plaza. "That was built only five years ago," he said. "Only the wealthiest of people can afford to stay there."

"It's all very grand," she replied, 'but it seems to depend on how much money you have. 'Do you have a big house? Do you have a motorcar? Can you stay in a fancy hotel?' Fred told me to read the novels of Horatio Alger. I couldn't find them anywhere, but he told me some of the stories. They're all about people moving from rags to riches, and success is counted only materially. This city—it seems it's all about being the biggest and the best. There's nothing about you becoming a better person or remaining true to yourself but poor." She stopped, hearing a note of resentment creep into her voice.

Niall turned. "I'm so sorry. I was just trying to show you New York without mentioning Fred. I wasn't actually saying anything about money."

"I'm sorry, too." She looked across at him, seeing him properly for the first time in a while. "I know you're only trying to make me feel better. I'm not taking any of this in, really, and Fred didn't live here, anyway. He lived in Philadelphia. It's just that all this commotion, the discordant roar of the city, makes me feel gloomy."

"I can take you to Macy's, a department store, if you like so you can get an idea of where he worked. And it's quite near the station where we have to get a train this evening. It's not exactly like the one he worked in, but it'll give you an idea. But first, we may as well go into the park as we're here, and it cushions you from the noises of the city."

Niamh gave in, and they strolled into the park, stopping by the lake to eat sandwiches bought by Niall. It was still quite cold in the March air, the trees only beginning to get their leaves back, but it was quieter than on the street. They walked as far as the Metropolitan Museum of Art, an imposing building with huge columns that fronted Fifth Avenue.

"I don't think we have time to look in here and Macy's. I fear it's one or the other, but it's entirely up to you," said Niall, who constantly seemed attentive to her wishes. "You can either see paintings you can only look at or stuff that you can afford to buy."

"I think that if Fred had been here, I would have twisted his arm and gone to the gallery."

"If that's what you want to do, then we should go."

"I don't know. Maybe it would be a good idea to see the kind of place he worked in. But then again, it's not the actual store, and I've read about this museum."

"Come on. I've never been into the museum either, and I lived in New York for six months. I think it's what Fred would have wanted. He loved to talk about the way you knew everything about books and art and history."

Niamh could feel herself beginning to cry again, but she shook it off and said, "All right, let's go in."

It was like a palace to art. The entrance hall was huge with great stairs taking you up to see paintings from every century, some very old and some more recent, like the Manet. This time, she was entranced but for a different reason; and for a while, she forgot the wretched feeling that Fred was no longer here, and she was instead captivated by the beauty in front of her. They ended the visit with a cup of tea.

"I think Fred would have liked the museum, but he would have hated this tea," said Niall.

Niamh laughed, feeling slightly more at ease with Fred's best friend.

"They haven't got the hang of brewing it," he added.

"No, they haven't. It's like dishwater."

As they walked back down Fifth Avenue, Niamh stopped as they came to St. Patrick's Cathedral.

"Would you mind if we went in?"

"Not at all. Anything you want to do."

"I just wanted to light a candle for him."

"Anything."

They walked into the church with vaulted ceilings. It contained a solemn peace away from the clattering of buses and horses and motorcars, the sheer hustle and bustle of the busy city.

Niamh lit the candle, which flickered, while she attempted to pray; but the flame seemed as hesitant as she was in her devotions. She looked over to Niall.

"Let's go."

"Are you sure?"

"I just feel robbed all the time. Angry. I just want to scream at God and ask why? Why did You have to kill him?" Her voice was raised. "Sorry," she said, dropping it. "I don't even know you, and I'm saying things that I haven't said to anyone."

"It's all right. Sometimes, it's easier to say things to strangers than it is to those who you are close to. Say what you like. You won't be judged by me, at least," he said, in a tone that spoke of true sympathy and real commiseration. "I've felt a fair few things like that myself, and I wasn't about to marry him!"

"I haven't really stopped since I heard. I was so busy getting everything ready to go, and I couldn't say anything to Padraig and Sinead on the ship. So, I just went on turning it over and over until I couldn't think anymore. I thought lighting a candle would make me focus on Fred, but it didn't."

"It just made you resent God more."

"That's it. That's exactly what it did, and I just can't bear it."

"I hate to say this; but we had better get moving, or else, we'll miss the train. But I can tell you a funny story about him, if that would help."

"I think I would like that."

"I'll tell you when we get on the train. We've a long journey ahead of us."

As they settled down with their bags stowed away in the racks above, Niall began his story of Fred.

"It was when we'd been in Mace about three weeks. What do you know about Mace?"

"I know it's a mining town in Idaho, and there isn't much to it. And I know that Fred thought that the mountains around it were breathtakingly beautiful. And I also know that it was mainly men who lived there."

"Ah, yes. That's true. But there were women there, too, who, shall we say, were of a colorful variety."

"He didn't write about them," Niamh said, slightly taken aback.

"You don't need to worry. Fred was virtue personified, but most of the men were not."

"And?" she said, wanting him to continue.

"Well, the men of Mace were—how shall I put it—robust in everything they wanted—be it money, drink, or women—and they were prepared to fight off anyone who challenged them."

Niamh began to relax as he set the scene for a tale.

"Well, as I said before, we'd been in Mace for about three weeks and were beginning to know some of the men in more than a passing fashion, but there were others who we knew well enough but did our best to avoid. One of them was Big Jim Wilson, so called because of his enormous bulk and fierce temper. What we didn't know was that there was a certain woman he liked to consort with so much that he thought of her as his."

"Nice to see the women are bits of property like the silver," Niamh interjected.

"Fred said you were a keen suffragist. Let me tell you, these men had no sympathy with suffragists at all. In fact, most of them probably hadn't even heard of women's rights, and that was certainly true of Big Jim—even if it wasn't for Fred," he hastily pointed out.

"Anyway, we had just returned from the mine and decided to stop for a drink before going upstairs when who should start talking to us but Molly, the apple of Big Jim's eye. She really didn't say much—was just passing the time of day and asking us where we were from— when Big Jim burst in through the doors and saw the three of us in a conversation that he decided was wholly unsuitable."

"What happened?" Niamh asked.

"Well, he was furious, spitting with rage. 'Why are you talking to these hoodlums?' he bellowed. 'You're mine.' Now, you may have heard the term 'the Wild West,' and at that moment, it certainly was. Many of the men, the American men, walk around with guns in holsters."

"Oh, my goodness. Fred certainly didn't tell me that. I was afraid of his being in a mining accident or eaten by wolves. I didn't think about him being shot!"

"You don't have to worry. As Big Jim went for his gun calm as you like, Fred, ignoring that Big Jim was going to shoot us both, put out his hand as if to shake Big Jim's. 'Pleased to meet you, sir,' he said. 'I'm Fred, and this is Niall. We're new here and were just asking your fine lady about the place, but now, we're going upstairs.' And quick as you please, he grabbed his hat and beat a hasty retreat before Big Jim had a chance to react. Honestly, that man had a real touch of the blarney."

For the first time, Niamh remembered Fred for who he was. Niall's story conjured a picture of him that she could relate to. Not that she had ever been in a situation like that with Fred, but in Niall's telling of it, she had imagined what Fred would do and so, for an instant, brought him back to life.

"Thank you for that," she said and turned to look out the window, recreating Fred in her mind.

The rhythm and sound of the train lulled her to sleep as they trundled through the night and into the morning, eventually getting to Chicago in the early evening of the following day. She had taken several books to keep her going on the journey, but she couldn't concentrate fully enough and spent much of the day just gazing out across the landscape, barely taking in the towns through which they passed.

Niall didn't intrude but drifted off to sleep, occasionally waking and staring out of the window. Once in Chicago, Niall sprang into action, took her bags down, and slung his over his shoulder.

"We're getting off here and catching another train in the morning," he said.

"Fred organized all this, didn't he?"

"He did. He wanted to introduce you to America in style. We're going to the Palmer House, which is another big hotel. I think he wanted you to know what it could be like before you got to Spokane, which isn't quite as grand and, I hasten to add, not quite as wild as Mace."

She smiled and then hesitated before she spoke again.

Niall interrupted the pause. "It's not that he wanted to impress you with money; it's more that he wanted to show you what he had achieved since he left."

Tears started to trickle down her face. "It was just him I wanted. Just him."

"I know; I know." Niall wanted so much to comfort her but knew that nothing he said would help. "And he desperately wanted you, too, but he was so pleased to have made enough to have you comfortable as well as over here. Perhaps you could enjoy it for how it was meant to be."

"The trouble is I can't help thinking that if he had only waited and saved up the money in that store, I would be seeing him rather than some empty legacy of flash hotels."

"But if you had done that," Niall added gently, pricked, too, by a sense of guilt for having persuaded Fred, "you wouldn't have been with the optimistic man who believed everything would work out in the end."

Niamh had to agree as she wiped the tears away and, taking a deep breath, said, "You are right, of course. Come on and take me to this hotel, then."

As the journey continued, a certain heaviness overtook her. It wasn't exactly a depression, more a tiredness of spirit that reduced the scenery around her to mere hills and trees and plains. As the train began to climb up into the Rockies with its spectacular peaks and valleys, she saw one mountain after another, vast but also empty, hollow, and lonely.

At last, they arrived in Mace.

"Could you take me to the mine where he died now, after we've put the bags in the hotel? I think I want to get it over and done with," Niamh asked.

"Are you sure?"

"Yes. I know I won't really be able to see anything, but I'd like to go to the place all the same. I think it's important somehow. And I'd like to see the room where you lived, too."

"I'll show you that first, then, as there's only one hotel in town, and that's where we stayed. Who knows? We might meet Big Jim!" he added, trying to lighten the feeling of depression, which was inevitably there.

Niall took her along to the hotel, passing a school on the way. "Fred sometimes wondered if you would like to teach there and how different it would be from what you were used to."

"I think it's probably like the one my father teaches in."

"Maybe it is. Maybe. So, this is the hotel."

It was slightly larger than the houses along the street but still built all of wood. Niamh paused. Fred had gone in and out of these doors a hundred times, had laughed and joked with Niall, looking forward to the day she would arrive—and now, here she was. He was so close, she felt that he might walk out of the door again and greet her; but then she remembered that he was never going to do that again. Fred was dead.

The misery of it all hit her, and she started to cry silently and then louder until the sobs almost choked her.

"I can't do this," she said, her hands in front of her face. "I can't. It's too awful."

"I know it is," said Niall gently. "I know." He hugged her and let her cry on his shoulder.

It seemed like an eternity but was only a few minutes before he gently pushed her away. "We're here now, so we may as well go in." Taking her by the arm, he walked through the entrance and then, after speaking to the man behind the desk, took her up the stairs to the room that he and Fred had shared.

Niamh went to the window. "He wrote me a letter about the view from here and a bit about how he'd seen a deer up in the mountains. He said it reminded him of the Garden of Eden, nature untrammeled."

"He often waxed poetic about it all. He really wanted you to see it and experience it in the way he had."

"I'm glad I've come and had a chance to be where he was, but without him, all I can see is that the mountains dwarf us. It's all so desolate and not spectacular or glorious at all."

"He thought they were sublime. I think that was the word," Niall said.

Niamh nodded. "We had a conversation about it when we were at Giant's Causeway—the wonder and fear of nature." She half-smiled and added, "I know it's probably the grief, but I can see only the fear." She turned back. "Just bleak cliff faces and gray rocks." She sighed and sat down on the crooked, wooden chair by the window.

"Yeah, I grew up near there," said Niall. "I know exactly what you mean. It can be a melancholy place, almost as if it's haunted, but it's beautiful, nevertheless."

"Exactly, exactly. And now, I think I would see only tragedy in the scenery." She paused, looking out of the window. "Like I see here." Adding so softly again, she said, "Like I see here."

Niall waited a few moments, watching Niamh wrapped around in sorrow like a caterpillar entombed in a chrysalis. "Do you still want to go up to the mine?" he asked tentatively.

Niamh looked up with an all-encompassing sadness. "I think I have to."

They walked silently up to the mine, the dirt sticking to her shoes, her skirt weighed down, laden with the mud.

"So, this is where it happened. Above ground."

She looked up at a hissing and clanking contraption carrying black, dripping sludge mingled with the rubble of hard, unforgiving rock, the only part of the mine that she could see.

"Yes, there was a problem with the conveyor belt and lift shaft over there, you see." He spoke purposefully, as if deliberately telling her how it actually happened at the place where it actually happened might, in some way, help. "That takes all the slurry out of the mine," he continued, watching her all the while he was saying it. "And he was trying to fix it when a wire shook loose and electrocuted the whole thing. It was so quick, he didn't even cry out."

Niamh stared ahead and said, "You know, when he said he was going to go, I was so afraid he was going to be buried alive—and I'm glad he wasn't—but still, it's a terrible way to die."

"It is." He continued to stand as Niamh struggled to take it in. The finality of it. At last, she turned. "Come on, we'd better go to the hotel."

They wound their way back, leaving the huge machine wheezing and groaning, back down through the town. They talked little.

In the morning, they caught the train again, this time to Spokane and then to the graveyard. They found a plan of the cemetery and walked to where Fred was buried. There was only a mound of earth.

"I didn't have time to get him a gravestone," said Niall. "I'm so sorry. But he will have one. I promise."

Niamh knelt down and rested her palm on the earth. Tears welled once more.

"Fred, oh, Fred." All that drive, that ambition, that irrepressible optimism finished by a loose wire touching a conveyor belt. A surge of electric energy and then nothing. Ended.

"Goodbye," she whispered and then rose. She turned and saw Niall brush his cheek.

"What do you want on the gravestone?" he asked, collecting himself.

"Put that he was electrocuted."

"Are you sure?"

"Yes. I want people to know that it was sudden. I want people to know when they look at his grave in years to come that he didn't die of disease—of consumption or something—but that he was taken away from us, robbed of him in a way we didn't expect. Will you do that?"

"Of course, I will, if that's what you want."

"It is."

She turned and looked down at the grave and, tearing herself away from it, said, "Let's go. I feel as if I want to lie down beside him and stay here forever, but I can't. I have to get back."

"You can stay on a few days if you want. The Hotel Spokane will extend your stay as long as you want."

"I'm sure, but I have to go. The only reason I was coming was to be with Fred, and now that he's not here, I have no reason to stay. Prolonging it will only make me sadder." And taking one final glance at the grave, she said, "It's heartbreaking enough as it is, but now, I can always say I've been here and seen where he died."

Niall nodded. "I'll get the gravestone done just as you wanted. Are you sure you don't want to appear on it? Beloved of Niamh?"

She shook her head. "If we were married, maybe. But we weren't. It would seem odd. Besides, he's the one we want to remember, not me." They walked back to the hotel without speaking again.

Niamh took one last long look at the dizzying heights of New York and the hope that it had promised. The deep groan of the horn sounded as the ship moved slowly out of the harbor, sailing past the Statue of Liberty, her face impassive, out onto the Atlantic Ocean that would take her home.

Present Day

New York City, USA

When Megan Anderson told her two daughters, Lowri and Rhiannon, they could accompany her on a trip to New York, they were delighted. They had been to New York only once before for her mother's, (the girls' grandmother) eightieth birthday. Actually, her birthday had been in Vermont, but they had gone to Woodstock by way of New York, where they had stayed near the center of Manhattan.

On that occasion, they had done some of the main tourist sites—the Empire State Building, the Guggenheim, the Metropolitan Museum, and the Museum of Modern Art. They'd been to the Museum of Natural History, seen Broadway and Time Square at night with all its billboards lit up, blinking in gaudy technicolor. They'd eaten an ice cream in Washington Square and been into the lobby of the Chelsea Hotel, where it listed all the famous people who had died there or at least visited—Dylan Thomas and Sid and Nancy.

They had walked for miles. In fact, they had walked so far that Lowri had developed a flu bug. They had walked from the hotel all the way down to the Empire State Building early in the morning, and she didn't feel well enough to stand in all the queues to get to the top. She'd said as much in the hotel, but her father had insisted; and in the end, she was glad she had gone. It was an amazing view. It was so high, you felt that you were on an airplane, everything below like ants—not that you could see people really; you could barely see cars.

They'd been to the shops, as well—the huge department stores like Bloomingdale's and Macy's and the more specialist ones that just sold clothes like Barneys. Bloomingdale's even had a musical evening where they had the stars of Broadway shows turning up and singing numbers from them. It was dazzling.

They hadn't been to see the Statue of Liberty, though, or Ellis Island; and they hadn't been to the zoo in the Bronx. Rhiannon was very keen on zoos. She'd been to the one in Central Park with her father, while Megan and Lowri had gone to the Met. They'd met up later. So, this time, they were going to go to all of the places they'd missed the first time.

Megan was there for a conference. It was in the Jesuit University of Fordham, which was actually in the Bronx, so they had arranged to meet up there after she had showed her face in a number of the sessions. It was the first time they had used public transport in the States, as well. Megan hadn't wanted to stay at the university as it was too far out of Manhattan and she wanted the girls to have a good time in the Big Apple.

Staying out in the Bronx would have meant too much traveling on the train, and she was slightly apprehensive about the Bronx, anyway. The university was just by Fordham Station, but nevertheless, she wasn't that comfortable commuting backward and forward to the city. One journey for the girls would be enough—to see the zoo. She had researched where to stay in Manhattan, as well, and in the end, she found a hotel right on top of Grand Central Station. Fordham was a thirty-minute ride from there.

She left them sleeping; she was still jetlagged enough that the early start didn't worry her that much. She navigated Grand Central Station and found the train she wanted. It was strange that the platforms were below the main concourse of the station, which was vast; look up, and you could see the zodiac on the ceiling high above.

Sitting on the train, clutching her book, and emerging out into the light, she noticed how the areas of New York changed from the affluent into poverty, through Harlem and the huge projects and on to the Bronx. Once out of the subway, you were again confronted by poverty—perhaps not at its most extreme but poverty, nevertheless. Yet opposite the subway was the gated Fordham campus. Within minutes, she was meandering through parkways with stately Edwardian-looking buildings on either side supporting names like Loyola.

The girls came and met their mother at two and grabbed a lunch, which was not actually theirs to have, not having paid for the conference—but no one seemed to mind. They walked to the zoo. It was about only twenty minutes, but they had to cross some serious highways to get there.

Megan dimly remembered something about a Robert Moses designing vast parkways to circle New York. Whether or not this was one of them was unclear, but it certainly discouraged walking.

They spent a pleasant afternoon looking at the animals in the large park that made up the Bronx Zoo. They also spotted a group of Amish teenagers or, possibly, Mennonites. All the girls' hair was knotted away, hidden within a cap, and their clothes were traditional, smocked dresses. It was so unusual that they stood out; visitors at the zoo gave them a wide birth and then looked back at them as they passed.

Megan wondered if they might have been Amish on Rumspringa, that period when the community let young people loose to decide whether or not they were committed enough to join the flock or not. If they refused, they were cast out forever, unable to connect with anyone in the community again. It seemed so harsh. Apparently, it was rare that they actually moved away from home, so perhaps they were Mennonite after all, still strict but slightly more integrated into the American way of life.

Strange that America had these sects, an extreme form of Protestantism that refused to come into the modern world. The Amish didn't have cars or electricity; even zippers were forbidden. Most of what she knew about the Amish, she had to confess, came from the film *The Witness*, which wasn't a great source of information. A world within a world, connected yet cut off at the same time.

Day two was similar to the previous day with the conference in the morning and sightseeing in the afternoon. Megan had felt obliged to attend the conference once more, and to be fair, she was giving a paper jointly with another academic. Not that she had any idea what he was going to say. It was meant to be one that they had written together; but although she had sent him her part, he had never sent his back. And he wasn't at the first day of the conference, which was even more alarming.

In the end, he turned up with about five minutes to spare and gave the talk that he always gave, virtually unchanged from the previous three occasions she had heard him speak. The Americans were all very keen on it, though. Clearly, they had not heard it all before. She was now done with the conference, and Manhattan awaited.

This time, the three of them explored Central Park more fully. Rhiannon had her portrait, or rather a comic book version of her, painted as they set out across the park. She had just broken up with her boyfriend of two years and needed cheering. Megan tried to tell her that it was almost inevitable to finish with someone once you started at university and had, in fact, done quite well in that it had lasted almost the full year. But this was of little comfort.

They walked to the place in the middle of the park where they had filmed *One Fine Day* with a terrace above and a fountain below. They saw busking like they'd never seen before, people doing fantastic pieces of acrobatics, and an amazing a cappella group, who sang beneath the terrace, the music echoing, resonating under the arches toward the fountain.

They left the third day for exploring New York's islands. Megan had thought she would see the Statue of Liberty on a previous visit. Someone had told her, when she had come a couple of years ago for another conference, that she just had to get the Staten Island ferry for free, and it would take her there. It certainly took her to Staten Island but not to the Statue of Liberty. Admittedly, she got a closer view of it—but not much, as the boat sailed past at speed.

A number of other people had been told the same thing. She saw an Australian, who happened, so it turned out, to be going to the same conference, muttering bitterly under her breath that she'd have paid the ten dollars to see the Statue of Liberty if she'd have known that this was the view she was going to get.

So, this time, Megan was going to pay the money, though not to go up the statue. That seemed going a bit far. She would pay extra to go onto Ellis Island, however. Some friends of theirs had been there the year before and recommended it. Apparently, there was a museum there that took you through what someone emigrating to the States would have been through and looked at the various influxes of immigration that took place at the end of the nineteenth and beginning of the twentieth centuries.

This time, they were going to grapple with the subway. Different subways in different countries felt odd. The one in New York seemed grubby and clunky compared to the one in London, and the fare system was just peculiar. Someone had explained they could just buy one ticket and then keep passing it back over the turnstile so they could all get in. So, they bought one ticket for fifteen dollars and hoped for the best. Every time the turnstile clicked one of them through, they couldn't help feeling that, in some way, they were defrauding the system; but if that was how it worked, that was how it worked.

They emerged again at Battery Park and made their way to the ferry terminal, where they joined a lengthy queue.

"This better be worth it," Rhiannon said.

"It will be, honestly. Emma and Amy loved it, and their dad said it was a very inspiring experience seeing all those immigrants' first encounters with the U.S.," Megan explained.

"I expect it's just one great publicity stunt on behalf of the U.S. government. 'Look how benign we are. We take you from wherever you are, whatever the circumstances. We are your friend,'" said Lowri.

"They may have cleaned it up slightly, but it'll still be worth going. You had a relative who went through Ellis Island, I think. We can look it up when we get there. I think there's somewhere you can check if you know someone who emigrated to America. Gordon told me about it."

"I didn't know we had someone in our family who'd gone to America. Who was it?" Rhiannon asked.

"It was your great-great uncle Fred Anderson. Your grandfather was named after him."

"Oh, so he was on the Irish side then," Lowri added.

"Yes. I think he came over because he'd just split up from his girlfriend."

"Seems everyone in this family comes to the States with a broken heart, then. Poor guy," muttered Rhiannon.

They had, by now, almost reached the front of the queue. Megan bought the tickets for everyone. The conversation drifted as they boarded the ferry and looked back at the place they had just left, a city crammed onto a small island reaching up toward the sky. They came up to Liberty Island quite quickly and looked up at the woman standing there holding a torch, to hope, to freedom, to a new beginning.

As they got closer, they couldn't see all of her as she towered over the boat. They had to crane their necks to get a sense of her full height and stature.

"You know, she was sent over by the French. A fellow revolutionary country. She's not really American at all. She's European," said Rhiannon.

"A surprising historic fact from you," Lowri quipped.

"I do study history, you know," snapped Rhiannon.

"Yes, I know, but you don't often let it show!" Lowri laughed as Rhiannon glowered at her.

"Come on now, you two, come on. Enough of the quarreling. We're on Liberty Island—home of the free. Let's take a look around before we get the next ferry," Megan said as they stepped onto the small quay.

They walked around the base of the statue and saw where you could go in to climb it. They looked up and saw tourists way up within the crown she was wearing.

"I'm glad I'm not up there. All you can do is look down, and it's way too high to be doing that," said Rhiannon.

"You'd get a good view of New York, though," said Lowri.

"True, but I can see it perfectly well from the ground, thank you very much," Rhiannon replied.

"It's strange when you get up close to it, isn't it? It's like an exotically designed skyscraper, really," reflected Megan.

"What do you mean?" they both asked simultaneously.

"Well, it has lifts and windows and stuff, just like the buildings over there. It's just that it's designed to be a woman."

"When you look at it like that, I suppose you're right. Can we go to the gift shop? I've seen people wearing those foam crowns, and I think I want to embrace the ridiculous," Rhiannon said.

Soon after, armed with the foam crowns and looking reasonably absurd, they queued for the ferry to take them to Ellis Island.

"So, what's this about that man called Fred, anyway?" asked Rhiannon.

"He came over about 1907, I think. I don't know much about him, other than his sister kept all the letters he sent home from the States. He was there about only nine months, and then he died."

"Died!" Lowri exclaimed.

"Yes. As I recall, he was in a mining accident or something. I seem to remember he's buried in Spokane, Washington. A friend of Dadcu's went there and took a picture of his grave."

"That's really sad. You mean, he was sent to the States and died nine months later? That's just awful."

They were about to dock on Ellis Island. Knowing that someone connected to them had made the same journey caused them to look at the building differently. Knowing that the same person had lived only nine months after he had first landed here gave the imposing Victorian building a more somber, almost melancholic feel.

They walked up to the main entrance hall and tried to imagine what it must have seemed like a hundred years ago, crowded with people trying to get into the country, leaving who-knows-what behind. It was not that the hall was empty now. There were plenty of visitors, some congregating around large posters telling them what used to go on, others just strolling through. But their voices just echoed in that great vault of a room.

The museum—because that was what it was, really—was spaced out over two floors. Most of the information was done through reading what the large display boards said about what had gone on in the particular room they were entering. There were a few exhibits, too, such as the instruments used for checking a person's health, particularly pink eye—or trachoma, as the poster said it was called. Everywhere, there were pictures of immigrants entering the U.S. There was an embedded optimism everywhere, even if it said life might be tough at first.

"I told you it was one huge rallying call for America," Lowri complained. "Look at these people—grindingly poor in Italy and even poorer once they got to the States. But does it say that anywhere? No, it does not."

"It's weird, though," mused Rhiannon, 'because something about coming to the U.S. must make you feel that life will be different. Otherwise, why bother going?"

"True, but look at that great uncle of ours," said Lowri. "Thought he was coming to the land of the free, going to make a fast buck in mining, and ends up dead nine months later, leaving everybody in Ireland heartbroken. His sister even kept his letters all those years."

"Do you know, I think we still have them—or, at least, Gu and Dadcu do," Megan said.

Rhiannon grinned. "I'd love to read them. I wonder if you'd learn anything from them or if they were just, 'Weather's great; how about yours?' I don't think they'd be that bland—she must have kept them for a reason—but maybe it was just because that was the last thing she had of him. I wonder if there's any from the girlfriend, too," she added. "That would be very sad, indeed. I wonder why they weren't allowed to be together."

"I believe she was a Catholic, and they were Brethren, so it was taboo," Megan replied.

"Oh, the joys of the Christian faith," exclaimed Lowri.

"You know, I could read his letters as part of a history project that we're meant to do over the summer," Rhiannon said. "We're meant to look at something from a historical point of view but use at least two original sources. If I could get what ship he went out on from here, and then use his letters and tie it into Irish history, that would be great."

They went back down to find out where you could look up someone who went through immigration at Ellis Island and found them in a room adjacent to the main hall. The room was covered in pictures of people piling off the ships, and two of them were of waiting in long lines. Some were close-ups of tired, beaten faces.

"Here we are," Rhiannon said. "You just have to put his name and the year you think he arrived."

"Well, it was Frederick Anderson, and I think it was 1907," said Megan.

"Okay. Well, here goes."

And there he was: "Frederick Anderson arrived in the spring of 1907 on the *Baltic*."

"I think they're in a folder down beside the desk. They're with all the stuff about the Andersons and your great-grandpa, Stuart Anderson."

Rhiannon's grandparents had moved just over a year ago into a flat in the city, their old house proving too big for just the two of them. For nearly forty years, they had lived in a Victorian rectory just outside Oxford. At first, it had been just a weekend home, her grandfather wanting somewhere that was separate from the tensions and pressures of his job in the civil service.

But then, when he hit fifty-two, he had changed direction altogether and taken a job in the university. His job had been in the trade office, negotiating between the unions and businesses, helping whichever government was in power talk to both sides. He'd written a couple of books on the subject and was often called upon to explain the nicer details on television. When they opened up a new business school at the university and offered him a professorship in industrial economics, it seemed like an opportunity too good to refuse. They already had a house nearby, and so what better than to move into the rectory fulltime?

It had been a difficult decision for her mother. She had always seen herself as a Londoner, despite her name; maybe she was just London-Welsh. That was her mother's doing. Betsan was very Welsh—Welsh parents, Welsh-speaking, brought up in West Wales. Her daughter was named after her grandmother, Megan, and had given the girls Welsh names, as well. She couldn't speak the language, though.

That was a cause of great bitterness on her part. Her father didn't want them speaking a language he couldn't understand, and Welsh was just too complicated for him to learn. Betsan spoke to her parents regularly, though, and so she grew up hearing it spoken often, grew familiar with its cadence and sound. So much so, that when they went on holiday every year to the seaside in Wales, she often understood what was being spoken, even though she didn't actually know precisely what was being said.

When Rhiannon and Lowri were born, their mother had insisted that they knew how to pronounce *ll*, the most difficult sound to replicate if you weren't a natural Welsh speaker. They both pronounced it perfectly. In fact, for the first three years of her life, until she went to nursery, Lowri thought the word for spoon was the Welsh *llwy*. There were other expressions their mother used, too, for which there weren't English equivalents, like *cwtch* and *twp* and *ach y fi* that she had passed on to her children so they used them, too.

Rhiannon had gone to a Welsh university. They were saturated in their Welshness. Lowri and Rhiannon even called their grandparents Gu and Dadcu, and Dadcu was Irish.

Rhiannon couldn't help but feel that Dadcu was secretly proud she was asking for the letters of her Irish relatives. She rooted around in the debris that was on top of, underneath, and beside the desk till eventually, she found the concertina folder.

"Hand it over, and we'll have a look," her grandfather said. "Here they are."

He revealed a whole pile of letters—about thirty of them—all packaged together.

"Hilda passed them on to my father when she died, and he kept them safe as well. Your mother met Hilda once when she was a very young girl."

"Did I? I don't remember," her mother said, surprised.

"Yes, it was in the early sixties. You would have been very little, about three or maybe four. She came over to see your grandfather. She must have been getting on at that point, certainly in her eighties. She was quite a formidable woman—very straightbacked, her hair always tied up in a bun. I was always a bit scared of her; she had that typical Northern Irish austere, dourness about her—very to the point, not blunt but ever so direct. She was very keen on women's rights all the way up to the day she died, and she never failed to bring any violation of them to your attention."

"Shame I can't remember her. She sounds impressive," Mother said.

"Yes, as I recall, she was one of the early suffragists in the North of Ireland, fought passionately for the right to vote all through the First World War. She'd have been really proud to know that her great-niece ended up working in a university still fighting the cause."

"I'd love to have met her now," Mother said. "I would have so much to ask her. So much."

"She went on fighting her whole life," Dadcu continued. "Her husband died in the war, and she never remarried. They had one child—a little girl called Mary, I think—but she died in the Spanish flu epidemic. She could have been only about ten or so. It was so hard to have lost everyone; but Hilda turned it around, got her qualifications, and became a teacher."

"That's amazing. So, she lived on her own until she died?" asked Rhiannon.

"No, I think she lived with one of her younger sisters—Agnes— but then Agnes died pretty young, too, so she was alone for the last fifteen or so years of her life. There was someone else called Niamh, too, who helped her when her daughter Mary died. I think it was through Niamh that she went back to school, which was fairly radical because Niamh was a Catholic. And by the time Niamh had moved in, Ireland had just been divided into a Catholic South and a Protestant North. The Irish Republican Army was active even then."

"I wonder if Niamh was Fred's Catholic girl," said Rhiannon. "Maybe that's what brought them together."

"I'm afraid I don't know, but she was a keen suffragist, too, just like Hilda—that much I do know."

"So, why do you have the letters, anyway, then?" asked Rhiannon, wanting the conversation to come back to her history project.

"You could write about your great-great-aunt, it seems to me. She sounds like a very remarkable woman, fighting for women's rights and getting the help of a Catholic when the barriers must have been considerable," replied Mother.

"Yes, but I don't have any original sources about her or her campaigns. I have them only about Fred, and he sounds pretty interesting, too."

"I'm named after him, you know," said Dadcu, the current Fred Anderson.

"Yes, Dadcu. I figured that one out on my own," Rhiannon teased.

"Maybe that could be your next project, finding out about the suffragists in Northern Ireland with your focus being Hilda," said Mother.

"Not everyone is a feminist academic, Mum. I'm more interested in American gangsters than the women's movement."

"That's *Scarface* for you. It's a work of fiction. These were real people who fought for your rights," chipped in Lowri, who had been sitting silently in the corner, reading.

"And I'm eternally grateful to them," returned Rhiannon, "but I have a specific project to do over the summer, and it includes weaving in original sources to a historical event. And I have the perfect one—immigration into the United States through my great-great-uncle Fred. I have the passage documents and now the letters. So, why did your father keep them as well as Hilda? And have you read them?"

"Do you know, I don't think I ever have," Dadcu said, thinking about it. "When you're done with them, I most certainly will."

"But you've kept them, too. I mean, as well as your father and aunt," Lowri said, finally becoming engaged in the conversation.

"Well, yes, by the time I got them, they were a piece of history, I suppose. Anyway, here they are. Please be careful with them. I realize—now that you have pointed it out—that I have never read them, but, as you also have made me aware"—his eyes twinkled as he said it—"they are a vital part of our story, my story." And with that, he passed the letters over to Rhiannon.

"I promise you I will take great care of them and return them to you soon."

19

Rhiannon had all the letters spread out in front of her on the kitchen table. She looked out the window at the Irish Sea. On a really clear day, you could see the Mountains of Mourne. If you followed the line from the Llyn peninsula past Bardsey Island, you could just detect the faintest hump on the horizon, the Mountains of Mourne. Ireland.

Rhiannon had never been to Ireland. This was as near as she ever got on her summer holidays in West Wales, staying near to where her grandmother grew up. She had been coming here since birth, staying in the cottage by the sea that her great-aunt had owned. Now, though, she was exploring the Irish side of her family through these letters, gazing across the waves to a place she had never seen.

She strained her eyes to see if she could catch a glimpse of the Irish coast, but today, she couldn't. There was a mist hanging over Cardigan Bay that meant you could barely see any of the Llyn, let alone Ireland. When she was small, her father used to joke that he was going to swim all the way to Ireland, and she had believed him. In fact, he merely swam to the buoy and back, which was, according to her mother, quite far enough.

She looked down at the letters again. Fred must have sent about one a week, given that he was there for only nine months. They weren't in any order she could tell because some were early on, and others were around January 1908. The first thing she had to do, then, was to create a timeline from the first to the last.

Picking them up, she felt an odd salience. The letters were written home, actually written by the man she was now investigating. These letters had passed through Fred's hands and been received at the other end by his sister Hilda. That was why she liked history and, in particular, the stuff on original sources. It was her way of connecting back to the past and the past reconnecting back to the future. It was her way of having a link with people in her past—a real link—in this case, through the letters on the kitchen table in front of her.

It took her longer than she had expected to sequence them chronologically. They were written in such small print and around the sides as well to use up all the space on the paper. The handwriting had begun to fade slightly, too, so that on occasion, it was hard to decipher what was being said. She wasn't really looking at the content for now, though, just when they were written.

She put them into three broad batches: the ones just after he arrived; the ones that described his life in Philadelphia, and then the ones out in Idaho. That was where the gap lay. It had obviously taken him some time to get to Idaho and then to find a postal service to send letters back to Ireland. Other than that short passage of time, he had faithfully written to Hilda once a week.

She couldn't really imagine what that must be like. The only time she'd been away from home was going to university, and at first, she'd found that very hard, almost impossible. After her mother and father had left her in her new room, she had cried and cried, wept into the duvet they had chosen together earlier in the summer. She had been afraid that she wasn't going to get to know anybody, make new friends, keep the old ones she had—and she hadn't managed that with Mike. In fact, she'd found it so hard that she developed insomnia in her first term there and even had to go to the doctor about it.

And yet it was so much easier for her. There was texting, video chats, email, and even phones. She called her mother virtually every day, and her sister almost as often. Everything was instant—showing everyone what you had eaten or the activities you'd done that day. The thought of going somewhere no one you knew had ever been and being able to send back letters only once a week was incredible, unbelievable—yet people back then did it all the time.

"How's it going?" asked Lowri, walking in from trying to sunbathe outside.

"Okay, I suppose. I haven't really started looking at them as yet. I mean, I've skimmed through to get a sense of them but not actually sat down and read them. And then I worked out what I'll say and which ones I'll include."

"I think you need to take a break and have a cup of tea with me in Evans. It is your holiday, after all."

Rhiannon agreed and so carefully stacked the letters in order before heading out to the café. Their mother joined them there, as well as their old friends Emma and Amy, who came down every year to the same seaside resort. Emma and Amy's mother, Fiona, and grandmother, Nest, were already there, saving a table for their group. Gordon, Fiona's husband, was apparently on a work call. It was the only way he could get away to West Wales for a break by being in constant touch via the internet or phone.

"So, what's this I hear about your ancestors?" asked Amy. "Found anything juicy or scandalous in the letters?"

Rhiannon laughed. "Nothing as yet, and I doubt I will. I've got only the letters he wrote to his sister, and I doubt he'll put in anything sensational in them. I'll let you know the minute I do, though."

"Hey, I think they can see a dolphin," said Lowri.

A group of people were standing on the other side of the road from the café, at the top of the path that wound its way down to the beach. They were all looking out to sea and pointing to a spot just beyond the buoys.

"There!" one of them exclaimed.

Lowri shouted, "Yes, it's there. In fact, I think there are two of them."

Mother and Rhiannon scoured the sea when suddenly, a dolphin broke up through the waves and turned around, flicking its fin as it did so.

"That was a pretty good view of a dolphin," said Mother. "You don't usually see them come so far out of the water as that."

"I remember two dolphins coming up very close to us when we were out near the buoy," said Rhiannon. "It was really scary."

"So much for swimming with dolphins, then," replied Lowri.

"They're much bigger than the ones in the States that people swim with down in Florida. These are the biggest in the world. Bottlenose. I tell you they were at least ten feet of leaping fish," said Rhiannon.

"Mammals," corrected Lowri.

"Yes, okay. But they were huge and so close. I can't tell you how quickly I swam away from them."

The sky was becoming overcast, and with it came a stiff breeze with the threat of rain.

"We better get back to our house before it starts to pour Mum," said Fiona.

Back in their own house, Megan volunteered her services to look over some of the letters; Lowri joined in.

"I think it would be good to read them together. It'll take an age to read them all through, and after all, we're all related to him."

So, they divided up the letters into the three categories Rhiannon had already found—the early letters, Philadelphia, and the West.

Rhiannon took the early letters, as that was what she thought she was most interested to look at, the whole process of immigration. She wanted to see if he had commented on it in any way or talked about the procedures when telling his sister. Lowri took the middle section, Philadelphia, mainly out of interest but also to see if there was something in them that explained why he'd suddenly left the comparative comfort of living in a big city and gone out West to cowboy country. That left Megan with the last part—mining.

It seemed ridiculous now, but when Megan had heard that Fred had died in a mining accident, she had always assumed it was coal. Coal was what you mined, and with all her Welsh family and a husband from South Yorkshire, coal mining made perfect sense. Her father-in-law had been the manager of a pit, and her brother-in-law had been first a miner and then a pit deputy. Mining meant coal, and the fact that he was mining at the turn of the twentieth century meant that accidents were not so uncommon. Pitheads collapsed; miners could become trapped. What she couldn't understand was why anyone would choose to go down a mine when you had a very nice job in a department store.

Reading the letters, though, she became aware he hadn't gone down a coal pit at all. He was mining for silver. It was his way of getting rich quick. Clearly, his sister had been anxious about his going, as the first letter from somewhere called Mace was full of reassurances that it wasn't nearly as bad as she feared.

"I think I've found out why he went," Lowri announced. "Our Fred was quite the entrepreneur. He's talking about a friend of his called Niall, who's gone out West and is making a fortune in the silver mines and has asked him to follow. There's something about his needing to make a lot of money fast so that he can pay for a ticket for someone called Niamh to come to the States."

"So, then it *was* Niamh he was in love with—the woman your great-aunt Hilda lived with. Isn't that the name Dadcu told us?" asked Rhiannon.

"Yes, I think it was, and she was the one who encouraged Hilda to go back to school after the war and get qualified to teach," replied Megan. "Let's see if we can find out any more."

"I've found a reference to Niamh in the first letter he wrote back to Hilda, asking if she would hug her for him. She must have known about the relationship, then, when the families disapproved, which says even more about her. Can you imagine what that must have been like, saying goodbye to someone who meant that much to you and not knowing when you would see them again? In her case, *never* seeing them again?"

"It's his optimism that gets me," said Megan. "Here he is, writing from the back end of beyond, and he's so clear that he'll see Niamh in just a few weeks. Listen to this.

Dear Hilda

The wait is nearly over. Niall and I have been incredibly lucky.
We've been mining up here in the mountains above Mace. There
are a few big mining companies in the area, but there are also
some smaller ones, too, and that's what we've got into. The area
was part of a thing called the Gold Rush, but it's all silver now.
They say even the silver's running out, too, but there is more than
enough for me and Niall. And now, I've turned the ore into hard
cash. I can get that ticket for Niamh to come out.

I don't think we'll live here anymore, though. It's fine for two men,
but I think Niamh deserves somewhere better than this, though I
think I'll stay out here in the West. It really is a new country out
here, away from the petty prejudices that have kept us apart for so
long. See, she has had to wait less than a year for us to be together
again. And don't worry—I'll break the news to our parents.

"I think that's the last letter he sent," finished Megan, putting it back
down on the table and spreading it out as if to signal its importance.

"Yet that cheerfulness was all so misplaced because about a week
later, he was dead," Lowri added. "I wonder if we can find out exactly
how he died."

"It's all just much too sad for words. It's a shame there are no
letters to Niamh and only to Hilda. Hilda must have known he was
writing to her, and they were still in touch years later. Maybe she just
couldn't bear to have them, or Hilda thought they were too intimate,
so she didn't like to ask. I suppose we'll never know," said Rhiannon.

"You can understand it. Hilda has kept the letters that were part of
her family's story, and although Niamh was, too, in a way, she never
became an Anderson," Megan concluded.

"Yes, but she lived with Hilda, didn't she, helped her get back on her feet after her husband and then daughter died?" Rhiannon added with feeling. "She sounds like she was more part of the family than any of her actual relations."

"Yes," chimed in Lowri. "She sounds like something of a feminist, too. Hilda went back to school because of her and became a teacher. I wonder what she was that encouraged her to do that."

"She may have been a teacher, too," answered Megan. "Being a teacher was a fairly respectable thing to be back then, and she obviously knew what to do, how to get to university. But if she had been to university herself, then she must have been one of the early graduates. You didn't have to go to college to become a teacher, but she could have."

"It's just so frustrating doing this," Rhiannon said, picking up a letter and then another. "I mean, you just end up with far more questions and only a few documents to help you answer them." She looked at the pile of letters in front of her and sighed. "I love dealing with original sources, but you could go on looking at them forever. It's like an enormous detective hunt. You track one thing down, and then another thing crops up—and this is meant to be only a small project for over the summer."

"I think you can say one thing, though; your great-grandfather was much more tolerant of Catholics than his parents," Megan said. "He didn't become one himself, but he always employed Catholics as well as Protestants, and he paid them the same wage, which was unusual in the '20s and '30s. Northern Ireland had just become a part of the U.K., and it was very, very Protestant. That's why there was such huge dissent from the Catholics. It must have been so hard to go from being in the majority to being a part of a minority who were not treated well at all."

"Dadcu said his father was close to Hilda. Maybe she influenced him," said Rhiannon.

"Maybe she did, along with Niamh. It's strange he didn't talk about her, but she must have been a presence in his life," Megan continued. "He even took over a hotel in Donegal, which is part of the South. He did it in the '50s before the troubles began, but still, it was a part of the Republic, not the U.K. He was quite vociferous about the Orange Order, too. Your gu and dadcu used to go over and stay there. They stopped when I was too young to remember, but your gu always tells the story of dressing your uncle Martyn in an orange shirt when he was about four and your great grandfather making her go and change it."

"He called his first daughter Mary, which is pretty Catholic—the Virgin Mary and all that," said Lowri.

"I think you could call a girl Mary and still be a Protestant, but yes, he did, though I think it might also have been after his niece. She was a Mary, too, don't forget."

"Yes, that's true. So, maybe she called her daughter Mary because it was the most acceptable Catholic name a Protestant could use." Lowri paused and added, "Returning to Frederick, if he was in Mace, which is in Idaho, why was he buried in Spokane, which is Washington?"

"I think we might be able to find that out, but I suspect it was the nearest big town," said Rhiannon. "You can find out all sorts of things these days. There's all those Ancestry websites, and you can link up to ones in the States. You may have to pay, but there is bound to be a newspaper notice or something."

"Is that your ever-so-nice way of asking if I'll foot the bill?"

"Well, you have to admit, you're as keen to know as we are."

"Okay. I'll pay, but I think now would be a good time to take a break."

Megan phoned her parents later on that evening. They were coming down to West Wales next week as they always did. Betsan said it helped her keep in touch with her roots. It was the only time, now that she spoke Welsh, explaining that she almost thought differently in the language. She said it was hard to describe to someone who was monolingual, but there were ways of constructing thought that were language-dependent, words and phrases that were just not translatable.

Megan knew something of this, despite being, as she bitterly acknowledged, monolingual. She had been very interested a while back in the poetry of Edward Thomas. She had linked the way he wrote to the verse form *cynghanedd*, which was a way of echoing the sounds of words within a verse. But it was also a kind of onomatopoeia at the same time. She didn't know if Edward Thomas actually spoke Welsh, but he was familiar with the form and his own poetry, which, in some ways, was very sound-dependent and contained many of the characteristics of *cynghanedd* within in it.

And yet it wasn't *cynghanedd*. To be able to actually get what *cynghanedd* was you had to hear it and understand it in Welsh. It was a verse form that was unique to the language, and even if you read a translation of a poem that had been written in that form, it wouldn't be the same, wouldn't absolutely capture the melancholic tones and

cadence of the poem in its original language. Megan had been to
an *Eisteddfod* a few years ago, where she had heard someone recite a
poem using *cynghanedd* for either the chair or the bard—she could
never remember which it was—and it was beautiful, had a wistful,
lilting quality so redolent of the Welsh language. That didn't mean
you would always sound like that, but she knew what her Welsh
grandfather meant when he said it was the language of Heaven.

What she really wanted to know, though, was more about her
great-uncle Frederick Anderson and if there was anything else her
father had remembered. There wasn't too much, but he did know a
bit about Hilda and his own father.

"I think she did have an effect on him," her father said. "She was
quite a character. She was more into women's rights than the rights
of Catholics, but she didn't care what you were if your rights were
being abused. If a man was hitting a woman, she was always there
to encourage them to report it. Even if the Catholics thought the
Royal Ulster Constabulary was not their friend, Hilda would fight for
their complaint to be heard and for the women to leave their abusive
husbands. She was an early pioneer of homes for battered women
before it even became fashionable, and she didn't care what their
religion was.

"She was all for the woman being treated as an equal," he went
on. "If they were being paid less than the men and if some men
were being paid more than others, she was the first to be on the case
of the employer. So, I think that your grandfather really believed

in that, too; and if he didn't, he wasn't going to argue the toss with his sister."

He was fascinated to hear, however, that they had found out something more about the girl Fred was banished from seeing again: that her name was Niamh and that it was the same woman who had helped Hilda all those years ago and even lived with her.

"It kind of makes sense, now that I think about it, that Hilda knew all along who the girl was and was so friendly with her. I suppose I was too young for Hilda to talk much to me about it, and your grandfather was only small when Fred died. I think he must have known, but it wasn't as important to him. He hadn't lived through it in the same way that Hilda had. Having his letters was his way of remembering his brother, not the fact that he had fallen in love with a Catholic girl."

"Why did Hilda give the letters to my grandfather in the first place?" Megan asked.

"I'm not sure. It could be that he was the next man in the family."

"That's a bit unlikely for such an ardent feminist."

"Stranger things have happened," her father said. "The family Bible will be handed down to your brother Martyn when I'm gone, even though he's not the oldest grandchild."

"Good to see the patriarchy is still alive and well in the Anderson household." Megan laughed.

"No, I think it's that he was the next one down. All her sisters died before she did, so I think he was just next. And she did have a special bond with him. She practically brought him up, or so he used to say. Your great-grandmother had got beyond it by then, after eleven children."

"I can see why she got into women's rights," Megan said. "Imagine your mother having eleven children. Poor thing."

As to why Fred was buried in Spokane, he had no answers, only knew that he'd been told it and that he'd been sent a photo of his grave.

"It was one of my colleagues at the university. You know, Dan. He had a conference or something at Whitmore in Walla Walla, Washington; and on a day off, he'd looked the cemetery up somewhere and found it. I could ask how he found out where he was buried if you like."

"Thanks. That'd be great. It might save an awful lot of time looking it up. It might even tell us why he was there."

HE DID FIND OUT AND called the next morning to tell them the website, but it didn't tell them that much. Megan looked at the very small obituary that Dan had found when he had visited Spokane. All it said was that Fred was a miner, living in Mace, and that he had been electrocuted. It also had a picture of the gravestone, which also told of the way he died.

"Well, at least he didn't die in a collapsed mine with the whole thing falling on his head," said Lowri.

"Yes, I think that must be the worst way to die—hearing the rumbling and all those rocks thundering down on top of you. That must be just awful. I can't bear thinking about it." Rhiannon shuddered.

"Then don't," replied Megan. "I don't think being electrocuted can have been great either."

"Quick, though, I suppose," said Lowri.

All three of them looked at the computer, as if hoping that it would provide some answers. Rhiannon turned away and looked out at the horizon. She followed the line from the Llyn, past Bardsey Island, and searched for the Mountains of Mourne. There, ever so faintly, she could see the outline of Ireland, dimly as if from the past. She looked back at the letters on the table. Fred was there, and yet only traces of him survived. Not the actual Fred but one caught from brief moments in the letters that he sent—fragments of a short life captured in what he chose to tell his sister. She looked up.

"Maybe I *will* do something on the women's movement in Northern Ireland, but not now. I'll still do Fred and immigration. I've got enough to do that, but I want to know more about Niamh, too. After all, she was the reason he went to the States in the first place and the reason he went to the mines. I can find out who she was through the census records if she lived with Hilda—or perhaps, there are records of the group that they were a part of. I feel we know only his side of the story."

"Maybe you can just use your imagination," said Lowri. "Imagine what they meant to each other. You'll never actually be able to know."

"I suppose not." And with that, she picked up the last letter, sitting on the top of the rest on the table and started to write.

More from Ambassador International

After Catherine Reed's husband dies, she moves back home in order to accept a new position as the teacher for the town's one-room schoolhouse. Samuel Harris has suffered his own loss and guilt has burdened him ever since. When his old flame comes back to town, he wonders if they can find healing together . . .

Evie Parker is plagued by a recurring nightmare from her childhood—who is the woman in her dream? What does it mean? A deathbed confession compels her to leave her home in Rhode Island and travel to the Territory of Alaska, where she struggles to unravel a past shrouded in mystery. Can she come through storms, both physical and emotional, to open her heart to true love?

Set in post WWII Ireland, this retelling of the Biblical story of Ruth is an incredible love story . . . with a twist. Elderly Sarah returns to her hometown of Adare, Ireland, with her daughter-in-law, Anna. The suffering that World War II brought them was unimaginable, but they still have each other. With all their loved ones killed in the war, the two women have nothing but a hope that one distant relative will help them. Will this new beginning bring the healing that both of them have prayed for?

Printed in Great Britain
by Amazon